DATE DUE

FEB 20 '98	

Growing
Through
the
Ugly

Growing Through the Ugly

A Novel

Diego Vázquez, Jr.

W. W. Norton & Company

New York   London

Copyright © 1997 by Diego Vázquez, Jr.

For information about permission to reproduce sections from this book,
write to Permissions, W. W. Norton & Company, Inc., 500 Fifth Avenue,
New York, NY 10110

The text of this book is composed in 10.5/15.5 Stempel Schneidler
with the display set in Citizen Bold
Composition by Crane Typesetting Service, Inc.
Manufacturing by Courier Companies, Inc.
Book design by BTD / Beth Tondreau
Photo on pages 2 and 16 © B. Tondreau

LIBRARY OF CONGRESS CATALOGING-IN-PUBLICATION DATA
Vázquez, Diego.
    Growing through the ugly : a novel / Diego Vázquez, Jr.
        p.   cm.
    ISBN 0-393-03963-3
    I. Title
PS3572.A987G7   1997
813'.54—dc20
                                                    96–25904
                                                        CIP

W. W. Norton & Company, Inc., 500 Fifth Avenue, New York, N.Y. 10110
http://www.wwnorton.com

W. W. Norton & Company Ltd., 10 Coptic Street, London WC1A 1PU

1 2 3 4 5 6 7 8 9 0

To Marjorie Lin Kyriopoulos

Grateful acknowledgment is made to the Jerome Foundation, Minnesota State Arts Board, and The Loft.

Parts of *Growing Through the Ugly* appeared in different form in *A View from the Loft*, The Loft, 1992; *Do You Know Me Now?*, Normandale Community College anthology, 1993; COLORS magazine, Four Colors Productions, 1993, under the title "Some Whispers Never Leave"; and *Speaking in Tongues*, The Loft, anthology 1994, under the title "Nam Paso."

Special acknowledgment is made to the Estate of Pablo Neruda for permission to reprint lines from "Cuerpo de Mujer" from *Selected Poems: A Bilingual Edition* (Houghton Mifflin, 1990). Originally published in England by Jonathan Cape, Ltd. First American edition by Delacorte Press, 1972.

M.L.K., your time, heart, soul, and support in helping to shape the "raw ugly" into something publishable will never be forgotten.

Thanks to Jill Bialosky for taking that leap of faith.

Growing
Through
the
Ugly

Growing
Through
the
Ugly

August 31, 1969. This is my first day of being dead but I want to return to my abuelita's house. Granny's little red brick casita. Memory is stuck inside this box with me. Soon there will be memorials, but I am the memory. Cold feet jumping on a hot fire. Memory shows me things in small fragmentary bursts. Funny thoughts tingle through my fingers. Me at six. Still chewing my toes. Then suddenly, the week before I turn fourteen, leaving El Paso for the last time. Today. A brief glimpse at the white colored brightness the day before yesterday. It is the third week after my eighteenth birthday.

This box is getting stuffed into the huge cargo bay of an old warhorse air carrier where memory stacks up like a bunch of old Sunday morning newspapers. Yellowed articles record that the best for me was during those too few years in El Paso. Yellowed articles with bold headlines detail the first day I am with abuelita, mi Nana Kika, at the Mercado Bustamante on Calle Paisano. Nothing has been written to tell why I leave home so soon, just before I turn fourteen. The desire to know more increases with each new murmur. I am just pieces now, but I am getting stronger.

1

Buzzy Digit Gets a Name

especialmente, *monarcas*

The importance

of butterflies

has to

do

with

their

offspring

growing

through

the

ugly

and

always

flying

away

beautiful.

Doña Kika Soldano

(translated by Buzzy Digit)

When I was six, I knew things. I knew the sound of strangers when they approached from behind. I knew you could eat potatoes with the skin if they got washed real good. Not so with jicama. If you eat jícama skin, it jangles the feel of the earth onto your tongue for days and days. I learned this from my grandmother, mi abuelita, Nana Kika.

Nana Kika sold tortillas de maíz and two choices of tamales all day, every day of the week, at the Mercado Bustamante on Calle Paisano in El Paso de Tejas. Six was an important age for all of her grandchildren because it marked our first trip to the mercado to help her work. Our abuelita was famous. Nana Kika would amplify a lecture on the importance of keeping our lengua in working order, insisting, "The best hope for keeping your mother tongue intact is in this marketplace." In my early Mexican Spanish, I always defined lengua as "beef tongue for dinner." La Doña Kika Soldano did not want our tongue boiled and lost in the puffy steam of this caldron de los Estados Norteños.

From the day I turned six until three months before I reached the small age of fourteen, my El Paso home was with her. Her three-story yellow house was a little rumbley sometimes because the Southern Pacific ran right off the backyard. It wasn't really a backyard. Maybe fifty feet, and one tree separated the back door from the railroad tracks. When cousins or friends came over to play they usually stayed in front of abuelita's "big yellow bird cage." Except for me. I was always drawn to the backyard. The adults would warn me not to lead any of their offspring toward the tracks. "Don't be playing on those tracks when you hear the trains coming." Then, of course, they would offer any one of numerous stories about a small child becoming a bundle of blood on the rails.

Nana Kika was gentle and great. My old skinny grandmother, with the eyes of a rain-charged mudslide and the hair of a snowstorm, had the tall sense of an old Ponderosa with broken limbs all about her. La Señora Kika Soldano was the Ponderosa loggers would leave stand after a clearing.

For years, abuelita appeared to me as the tallest woman on earth. My head reached her waist. She was just under five feet, seven inches tall but she towered over all her grandchildren. I was frail, with cream skin and round eyes like my mother. The dry mood of my darkness came from a lost father. Nana Kika was my father's mother. Whenever I walked with granny, I would hold her hand, believing she could see beyond the horizon. Beyond the dirt crusted Rocky Mountains.

I must rely on legend to transcribe my name. My real name is Bernadino Soldano Dysyadachek, Jr. But I've been Buzzy Digit since I was a child. The exact moment it began is lost for me. Abuelita Kika used to ask how many Juniors could one family stand. It is said my favorite books as a child were books about cats. Children's books called cats "pussies." When I said "pussies" it came out "boosie." My older cousins, who were farther along in their command of this New World englich, played on it. Boosie became pussey, busy, boogsie, booze, boozy, Buzzy. My mother's Chicago-Polish last name was a burden to all. They took Dysyadachek and turned it to Dissachikie, Disastick, Digitstick, digs shit, dig it, Digit . . . my cousins were kind. They decided against calling me a pussy that digs shit. They invented Buzzy Digit. Because my mother was from the Windy City, I decided my real birthplace was Chicago. A Chicago Chicano, Buzzy Digit.

Abuelita Kika was also a diplomat. When I claimed to be her favorite grandchild, she would smile and lift the gentle, dusty importance of my desire into a look in her eyes that would send me into storms of joy. In private, she assured me of my most favored status, though I was never able to get her to confirm this in public. All my cousins, who were direct descendants of Satan and not worthy of Nana Kika's affection, also considered themselves her favorite.

My abuelo, my grandfather the baker, died of a heart attack when I was three. Nana Kika often spoke of the gentle heart of her Don Pablo, her huge baker macho de hombre who had seeded her with nine children. He was struck at the panadería, his bakery, a few minutes after midnight as he prepared to bake bread for a November Wednesday morning in an old West Tejas smelting town. I don't remember abuelo, but his bakery and his land became a legacy that survived all the debts his sons piled up against their inheritance.

The wars of inheritance raged as soon as abuelo was put into the ground. Nana Kika had four sons who served this country during la Segunda Guerra. Only two saw combat. One died three days after coming home from Nazi Europe. The other, my father, came home with malaria and the horror of the siege on Guadalcanal. He saved himself from those horrors by abandoning his familia—all the familia, his two little girls, his tiny boy, and a disbelieving wife.

Two versions of my father's disappearance evolved. The first, and most prevalent, blamed his duty as a Marine medic on that island as having permanently stolen his soul. At family gatherings, an uncle or auntie would pat me on the head and whisper sorrow for my terrible fate. It was good for tips, too, because they would stuff money into my little palm, telling me his return from la Guerra had affected him in ways no one could know. They insisted it was not his lack of love for me that caused him to run, but rather the toll of too many bodies he could not fix. The terror this caused his inner world could not be mended.

The second and least talked about version of my

daddy's fugitive status involved our almost-teenaged cousin, Gloria. She was the first grandchild, the oldest cousin, and epileptic. Exactly one year after my grandfather died, my father took Gloria to her swimming lesson at the downtown Y. The sun rose, promising to cover the desert with more heat. In the early morning, my dad gave Gloria the ride to her final swimming lesson. He drove away with the top down on his latest "demo," a red Chevy Bel Air. Sixty-seven minutes after Gloria waved goodbye to my dad, Auntie Margie received the call that would affect all our lives for the rest of time. The young swimming instructor cried to my dearest tía, "Everyone thought Gloria was holding her breath under water. She was in the shallow end of the pool and all the other girls were doing the same thing. The others kept coming up for air, thinking Gloria was just ahead of them in going back under. They thought she was winning." When the instructor witnessed a color of purple contrition on our Gloria's face, it was already too late. The small puddle of chlorinated water had poured a flood into the territory of a young girl's life. The water forced itself into her lungs without waiting for her seizure to stop. The water took Gloria as a gift. Our oldest cousin, almost a teenage girl, had been taken back. Gloria became an angel.

Only one time did I hear Nana Kika mention my dad in the same breath with talk of Gloria's death. Only one time did I hear her say she thought it was the one ride that destroyed him. All the other excuses for his abandonment centered on the war. The second big war. I became a believer of the drowned version.

They say my mother is beautiful. But she abandoned me after my daddy ran, her brave heart broken and saddened. I only recall her screams. Once, some crazy ghost screaming from an abandoned graveyard made her slice the skin on my head with a jab from a broom handle. I locked myself in the bathroom and cried while my head dripped blood onto my hands. When she finally opened the door, the blood had dried. She told me it was nothing and not to say anything to Nana Kika. In most pictures, she has eyes that look like the desert green of small lizards. Abuelita said they were the deepest green she had ever seen. They were eyes that made people feel as if they were looking into the center of the ocean.

My grandmother spoke softly of my mom and dad. "Mi'jo, they were so pretty, O, pretty together. But the war ruined him. Tu padre signed up with those Marines without telling anyone. At seventeen, he was already filling prescriptions for Hidalgo's pharmacy. He told the Marines he was going to be a doctor so they made him a medic. Y tu mamá, mi hijito, tan hermosa, and so strong."

"But, abuelita, if she was so strong, why did she hit me and where is she now?"

"When your daddy ran away, she left with a Mexican painter from Chihuahua. After that, she met some writer, or poet, from Chile and they went back to his home in a place called Temuco. The last we heard was her letter telling us of a place called Antofagasta. It is the place on this earth where the sun is always the toughest. She said you will be sent for when they get settled."

"They" included my two older sisters. My mother pleaded with Nana Kika that girls needed to be with their mother much more than a boy did. Granny never turned away a child and this is how I came to live with her. I was one of many cousins who would ask Nana to be my mother.

I had a favorite dream during my first year of school. It gave me a second chance at choosing a mother. In waking, I told myself that since the first one was lousy, the next one would not have to be so pretty that her eyes need to be green. *I just want her eyes to see me when she looks at me. That will be fine. She can wear short dresses. I want her to walk with me. If she wants to hold my hand, I will let her. She can touch me in public. She can be old, like thirty-three. She can have dark hair, short ears, crooked nose, and wide soft lips. Her breath will be from the heart of a strawberry. And when I sleep, she will kiss me. If I wake from broken dreams, she will let me sleep with her. I can lay my head on the inside of her thighs, or her belly, or on her breast like I used to when I could put my lips on her nipples. She will let me sleep on her buttocks if I want. She will take me like the ocean returning to gather all its stranded creatures. Her skin can have sand in the pores, but her eyes will remain clear. She won't hit me with crazy broom handles when I cry. I promise to choose a mommy who will tell me it is not necessary* *for tears because she knows how to be funny. We will laugh at men's jokes. And, because she wants me to grow protective of her, she will tell me about men. Then, she will let me warn her about things she already knows. As the night gets darker, she will let me be her child.*

When I was six, I knew things.

II

Mercado

Nana Kika is from the angels who brought us to the border. She was firmemente, consistently determined to make us find our special guardians. When the last of the seven bakeries and the last of her equity from a big yellow house on the south side of the Franklin Mountains dissolved, abuelita went back to work. I was a poor student in a poor school in a poor frontier town. The teachers were bored with our Mejicano Spanish and could not reach me like my tough, skinny granny with the neon white hair and the most sparkling laugh.

When Doña Kika's sons depleted her tiny savings, greed covered these boys and their wives. Except for my dad, who jumped onto his isolated island home and never tried to blame anyone. His isolation cost me my heart. He left us all behind crowded with attorneys who never stopped sending raging divorce demands. I lost some cousins during the turbulent declarations of contempt. I lost a few aunties. Women whose smooth tender legs were blotted from the rights of la familia. Uncles cried nightly from rooftops. Their sons-of-a-baker's lips soaked with rum as their arms held onto hourly women. They gave up on their wives . . . soft birds singing about sons. Los hijos de Don Pablo rushed ruby red extemporaneous furies at the dull, bleached women who married them for a slice of Don Pablo's estate!

They got lost in a jungle of puterías, of whores. Nana Kika said those boys spent too much time and money con putas. It made them lose passion for their brides, who had, at one time, promised to let them stick it anywhere. While her boys grew uglier and stole Nana Kika's last centavos, mi abuelita de oro, my granny made of gold, got innovative.

Señora Bustamante, Nana Kika's comadre from twenty thousand lifetimes, arranged for abuelita to rent one of the most visible stalls in the Mercado Bustamante. Granny had only two fine slender hands, so her real strength was in selling tortillas y tamales that looked and smelled hecho en casa. Home made. But a business agreement with the real baker of the goods, Don Martín de Montana Street, kept it a secret. His hidden factory revealed important discoveries for the grandchildren who witnessed an early exposure to the conspiracy of adults. In the pieces of silence that bounce from secrets, Nana Kika and Don Martín reached their business agreements. Secretos of profit.

Don Martin was a giant with the roundest belly and the roundest face and the roundest smile and the roundest bald head a man could have. The first most-beautiful man I ever saw. Looking at him was like watching the night with a full moon and a million stars. He was full of everywhere. For the children in my family, meeting Don Martín was an event that rivaled that of waiting for presents on a December morning from el Santo.

Strange stories surround the grim assistant baker of Don Martín's hidden Montana Street factory. Chonte, a drunken gila monster, looked like a lizard but his moves were much more dangerous. My older cousins told stories about being at the young age where some kids can look like either a boy or a girl. And the ritual of being left alone with el Chonte. It only took a few minutes for him to coat the nipples of preteen girls with baker's yeast. It is a legend that girls who got it early from him would have sweet milk flowing from their breasts when they gave babies their nipples. If the lizard Chonte made a mistake, sticking the yeast on a boy, then the pobrecito would be certain to grow up to be a sissy.

History was big for us. All of my older relatives listened romantically when Nana Kika would demand, "We own more rights to this desert then estos Americanos want to admit. They even stole White Sands up in New Mexico so they could play with all their UFOs and kill all those innocent Japonéses. Buzzy, I know your dad hated fighting all those guys in Guadalcanal but you know what? He was still fighting a real war. He didn't hate those Japs. He hated their leaders. Now that these gavacho leaders have built that bomb right in our backyard what's to keep them from using it on us? Nothing! With the bombs that they own they are going to keep this land away from us for a thousand years. And watch, someday, just to make sure that no more of 'us' can cross la frontera, they will build a wall all across the desert like they did in China. But we were here first and those mad gavachos stole it from us . . . somos parte indio . . . all of my family has indio in them. We are not 'Spanish' just because we speak it. Those Cabroncitos robbed us, too, even worse than these gavachos at Fort Bliss, but at least we can say we are Mejicano."

But bigger history was made for us when we ate the biege leche quemada candy Nana Kika gave us. Her favorite candy. The fate of Nana Kika's El Paso grandchildren, when they turned six, was to help her work at the tortillería en el mercado. At the mercado, she took your hand and placed it on an ancient wagon with big, ugly wheels and a long, black handle. At one time, the old wagon might have been red, but by the time I saw it, it looked invisible. On my sixth birthday she pushed me through the most direct, yet discreet route to Don Martin's hidden factory. The path was familiar and boring until we passed the alley behind the house of the gavacho. The dirty gringo from Georgia, Leroy Harvay, who had shot and killed un negrito burglar on the front porch of his house one Thursday at ten-thirty in the morning. The Nazi Harvay was known for training killer dogs. Nana Kika stayed sharp and precise in warning me as we rolled quickly past his house. "Mi'jo, never go close to that man!"

Don Martín always conducted the indoctrination

of a new grandchild into the business world. The round Don Martín. Even his factory was round. Don Martín supervised the initial loading of the invisible wagon. Fresh tortillas and warm, soft tamales with secret ingredients. He stuffed a large round bottle in a wooden box and placed two blocks of dry ice wrapped in old rags into the box. His instructions were to not unwrap or touch the burning ice. "Because it can melt the fingers off your hand." Everything warm got covered in waxed paper, assorted pieces of old clothing, and pieces of cardboard. Each day included more than a dozen return trips to the factory. Nana Kika accompanied us only on our first trip. After that, she expected us to remember what to do. We were part of the routine.

On returning to her stall at the mercado, the warm goods were dropped into a large, insulated metal box, which kept them fresh and hot until they were sold. Nana Kika unloaded the specially wrapped bottle and placed it under the table where she sat most of the day. A false facade behind the counter gave new anglo shoppers the impression that her food was made on the premises. Anyone who has shopped more than once at Mercado Bustamante in the heart of the barrio segundo on the southwest side of El Paso, and each new grandchild after the first day of work, knew that Granny only sold the little corn miracles. Don Martín and his lizard assistant, the drunkard Chonte, took care of the rest.

Until I turned thirteen, my most important job was to get my grandmother's goods to market. I always had a desire to help her. I considered myself her most loyal and available grandchild. Abuelita's requests for help were necessary to me. All my older cousins from the "Red" Rosemary to the boy hating "Pulgas" seldom continued to make pick ups and deliveries with the invisible wagon. They would usually just stay in the stall with abuelita and help her cure the world of its blues. Along with spiritual assistance from the round bottle.

I was destined to travel every inch of the mercado. Once I saw it, I could no longer exist without the taste and feel of the daily, huge chunchunchun of life crowding and pushing its way into the lives of those who try to replenish a hunger for something beautiful and severe. The hunger of men whose stomachs were lined with the caked-blood memory of war. The hunger of motherhood shattered by boys returning from battles with broken eyes staring into a future of agony. The hunger of young, foreign, girls as their breasts fall between the hands of grim strangers who have paid for this affliction. The hunger of an old man as he watches teen girls running in their Catholic-school skirts. The hunger of a young boy being kissed under the light of small candles while the Salvation Army choir sings in the park. The daily hunger of a small world exploding with desire.

The effortless joke of my young life became an ugly laugh when I was caught alone with the lizard drunkard Chonte. It was almost the end of my second summer with abuelita at the mercado. I was seven years old. I knew how to read round clocks and I knew my days of the week. *It is four P.M. on a Friday. Don Martín is not at the factory. Chonte says to be quiet and stay still. He quickly lifts my shirt and places his left hand on my titty. Then his other hand grabs my other titty. The hand is holding a glob of baker's yeast. While he smears my chest, his big thing starts to show under his apron. It looks like it is watching me. I feel it touch me on my shoulder and his hard lizard hands are rubbing my titties. Everything in his power rubs its way onto me. I feel a hot splash on my neck and smell his sweaty, exhaustion. His beard looks muddy. I remember the face of a circus horse as it sleeps after having performed. Dreaming for a choice.* Chonte drops my shirt and whispers, "Esto es what makes the yeast rise." He never touched me again. He had too many children to choose from.

Outside, on the street, I swayed. The world had become nothing but brown desert dust. The beginning of the end for me was all the dust. Fear had arrived. It hid behind the seconds and minutes on the faces of clocks. At 4:19 P.M. on a Friday afternoon, the world stopped. I was trapped under a big, smelly, ugly foot counting dust for hours and hours. Chonte was the first person who led me to believe the plaza park preachers with their warnings on hand-painted signs, "The END is Near!"

The preachers in alligator park never stopped talking about the end of the world. On Sundays at three A.M., they could be heard screaming at the drunk soldiers who had jumped the fence in order to wrestle an alligator. "These animals are going to bite off your whorehouse dicks." Every soldier wrestling with his animal bride would jump, UFO-like, from that pool. The preachers would howl, "These alligators were put in this park by God so they can test any soldier who is returning from a night of whorehousing in Juarez. Presidente Brandy and an ally gator means one lost body part."

As the years passed and too much of the zone known as the "Preacher's end" surrounded me, I would run to the mercado to find my abuelita Kika in rampant dialogue with her comadres. They were always in the middle of endless conversations concerning their poached pain from the untold suffering inflicted on them by their sons and daughters. Their oral studies on the condition of our souls were sanctioned by cups filled from the bottle wrapped in dry ice. I would come alive with them and they were good at ignoring me, so I heard everything they said. Except for the time Señora Bustamante was talking about how she had started to use her fingers instead of waiting for him. When she saw me, the vieja Bustamante stopped talking and renamed me "Droopy." She said I always had sad eyes, even when I laughed. I wanted to tell her to go finger herself, but I wasn't sure what it meant. My Nana Kika said there was no room for new names. My cousins had taken to calling me ese Buzzie Digito, and she was certain that name would stick.

Summers with Nana Kika were pretty. Everything, except the drunk lizard and the grief of the prophets, had the ooze of dreams. Dreams that carried me home after the howls of dark invaders had motioned for my throat. Nothing compares to those first years. The world spoke to me in a West Tejas español, which was the clearest, slowest, and most perfect dialect on the planet. I studied death, stars, and my abuelita's tongue. Nana Kika had a large army of translators available for any ventures into the Norteños lengua. Whenever I asked her why she would not speak la english, her answer never varied. "We were here first." She would scratch her left ear and talk of a time when the only spoken tongue was her Mexican Spanish. "No, hijo. There is nothing but an invisible line dividing us from our people."

When I was ten and the end of summer was near, that bottle in the box saved my life. My routine with the invisible wagon was broken when Yolanda Bustamente forced me against the fence and kissed my tongue. After that, I found myself with shaking knees, pulling a squeaky old wagon into the territory of Leroy Harvay's killer dogs. One of Leroy's Nazi mongrels found my leg and sunk his teeth into the back of my left thigh. I immediately abandoned the idea of whapping the dog with tortillas or tossing a tamale to stop this mutt's trained response. In those full-kill moments, my two tiny arms grabbed the bottle from the wrap of towels and slapped dry ice into the mutt's mouth. As the four-legged Nazi singed his tongue, I broke the bottle over its bad brain and ran. I had been told stories of dogs stealing children so that they could be raised as animals. But this was not a steal. This was a kill. My pants were bloody rags and my left leg felt loose.

Nana Kika's sacred bottle was broken, so I returned

to the factory for a replacement. It was not simple because I had to listen to Don Martín give me his thoughts on the particular family history concerning my dad and my older cousins. "Buzzy, don't you know how hard it is to keep this bottle fresh? I can't tell you how long it takes to mix and blend and brew this. Because it takes a long time and it is a very secret recipe . . . it has some of the same medicine that that Coca Cola used to have before the government wouldn't let them keep making it. My abuelito gave me this old formula, which he swore that Coca Cola company stole parts of . . . difference with his was that he also blended in ron de una isla del Caribe, he would say, 'and that island rum is the strongest magic in the whole world if you mix it right,' and then he also used some special yerba. So once a week I have to go into Juarez into colonia Anapra and visit a curandera that makes a special yerba that I add to my mix. It is a lot of extra work, niño. But I do it so that me and your Nana Kika can stay healthy." He looks at me the way a priest does before offering Communion. "Niño, you are too young to be trying to do what your cousins used to do. Oye, at least they were teenagers when they first fooled me with that old pendejada of a perro story. This dog story is too old now. I know your daddy. I know how early he got started on that botella. Don't be starting so young, niño. Because this botella is just for when you are older. If you start tasting it right now it won't work . . . just bad things will happen."

"But, Don Martín, look at the back of my pants! I tell you for real, lo que pasó. I didn't drink that stuff. Besides, wow, I smelled it and I don't know how anybody can drink it . . . it smells like a gas station. I . . . I . . . had to use the bottle and the flaming ice to knock away that gavacho's killer dog."

Don Martin studied the drying blood behind my leg and whispered to God that someone should pay for this. He did not apologize to me for his disbelief. He replaced the contents of the protective box and sent me away. I thanked Don Martín and left him shaking his head.

At the mercado, when abuelita saw me torn and shattered, yet slowly pulling a full wagon, she screamed, "Sangre de Cristo, niño, que te pasó?"

"Blood of Christ!" I felt like a martyr. But my pants were sufficient protection against the jaws of the killer. There were no deep punctures. My deep hero wounds amounted to small scratches on my skin. I quickly decided to ride this wave of heroism as far as I could. First, I retold the Yolanda encounter in full detail and quickly discovered that was not the pathway to martyrdom. My granny's compassion dissolved as suddenly as the cheap Nazi mongrel took to my thigh. She said I was too young to worry about girls and warned Yolanda through me that she had better behave or her mother would be told.

The first piece of this puzzle came to life. Sometimes, adults say things to children that are meant for adults. Sometimes, they just say things that are meant for anyone nearby. I knew that Yolanda's mother would be told.

Nana Kika's scolding softened and my attention faded. She concluded that Leroy Harvay and I are both as goofy as each other, because, "los dos no saben . . . neither of us knows where we are going." I stood there, quietly thinking of the plaza park, plasma-donating prophets. And Señora Kika Soldano stated, loudly enough for all the mercado to hear my public flogging, how she wished that the madman Harvay with the trained killer Nazi mongrels had been stuffed into one of those ovens she was certain he had operated for the Germans. "Todos los judíos pobres got gassed so he could live and train dogs to kill in nuestros Estados Norteños." When she grew silent, I walked across the street in search of a preacher.

III

Little

League

I played my first game of Little League baseball two months before I turned eleven. Because Chonte had coated my nipples with yeast and squirted on my shoulders, I knew I was destined to become a sissy. But I wanted to keep it secret. I was not a good hitter during the real games, only at practice. I told the coach I needed glasses for game days and that Nana Kika couldn't afford to buy them. Coach questioned why my glasses weren't necessary at practice. I explained, like a doctor, that it's only a sometime condition. That I had no way of knowing when my vision would turn fuzzy. This started a few years of being tagged as "Fuzzy Buzzy." I assured him that once la Doña Kika had the money to buy my glasses I would wear them all the time. Coach was too busy with other problems to worry about my eyesight. His team was in its first year of wearing new uniforms from a new sponsor. He let me play, in spite of my vision. In dark red, bold letters, the three lines across the back of my new shirt spelled,

COMPANIA don MARTIN
Tortillas y Tamales
(fresh daily)

I played second base until Bucky Renterría recovered from his butterfingers enough to catch a ball once in a while. He was bigger than me and able to hit the ball far on game days. I was slow, small, and stupid when it came to hitting the ball. I stood at the plate during a game, surrounded by an advancing army. The drubbing advance stopped to observe my desperation. I was a bone standing at the plate holding a feather against the cannon shot of an opposing pitcher.

It was not a fair war. Swinging aimlessly at the marauding shot, I discussed death with myself. I did not react in time to make contact. My next swing began as the ball returned to the pitcher. I was too anxious to wait for a bad pitch. To walk for me was a rare deed. I swung at each pitch. Not good timing for a lead-off hitter. In practice, I was consistent and ordinary. But, on game days, my coach would tell me to look up a word, "impotence." I thought it meant extraordinary. Coach eventually hid me in right field and placed my bat last in the line-up.

During practice, it was easy for me to face our team pitchers. Even when the coach yelled at Jan Halso—our best pitcher—not to let up on me, I could still hit his best stuff. But, I never took practice with me. On game days, standing in the batter's box, I recognized the monster on the mound as a member of the other team and suddenly that marauding army would appear. Surrounded in the field with every weapon pointed at me, I waited impatiently for the massacre to begin.

I played on the same Little League team with most of the best players in town. Mando "Sluggo" Enriquez. Anselmo "Flaco" Vázquez. And the "Vikings," Jan and Gabby Halso. Jan was our team's tall, blonde pitcher. Gabby, the "baby Viking" was huge. He played first base and batted clean-up. Sluggo batted third and hit more home runs than Gabby. In our Little League they were known as "Papa Sluggo and his baby Viking."

The Halsos were the first family I knew who spoke something other than Spanish or English. They talked Norwegian, which always sounded Puerto Rican to me. Or Cuban. I would ask them to repeat themselves and then they would repeat themselves in English. We laughed a lot then because their language always surprised me. I would begin listening to them, thinking they were talking in Spanish.

Everyone who went to Jan and Gabby's house would eventually call Mrs. Halso "Mom." No one knew why. They just did. I wanted to, but always stopped short before the word left my mouth. Mr. and Mrs. Halso owned the flower shop where my Nana Kika Soldano shopped whenever an occasion arrived. There were five Halso boys, the products of a wise florist and a tin-voiced, fat, drunkard husband. The husband was as mean as the Nazi dogs. But he had no bite. The boys were my first friends outside the border of our barrio. Jan and Gabby were twelve and ten. Erik was nine and couldn't play on our team yet, although Coach dreamed of the day when Erik would be old enough. The old-timer viejo scouts said that this nine-year-old was going to be even better than his two older brothers. I didn't spend time with Yule and Siegi because they were only five and four. The five Halso boys became my brothers.

Mr. Flower Shop Halso hated everything. The army had recently retired him. Of all the brothers, Gabby looked like his dad the most. Two Santa Clauses in one family. Not much else was known about old man Halso because no one could get a question in when he talked. When he started preaching, his lips pouted scary stories of apostles falling for evil women. The best story he ever told was of a bigshot company president falling for the brown eyes of an adulterous young teen girl. The old-time executive falls in love with a mexicana who lives in the whore house. The aged man divorces his wife of a million years to marry the young backroom beauty. Eventually, the old exec becomes too sick to satisfy his young bride and she begins sneaking out at night for encounters with strangers. Old man Halso, who emphasized the terrible life of sin in which the girl lived prior to meeting her savior, instructed us, "Once a whore, always a whore."

Mrs. Halso would interrupt, shaking her head, "You just can't be too sure. I don't believe that's true."

The man dies and leaves the young girl nothing. She returns to the old courts of enriched houses built for the satisfaction of men. She never again finds a man who can satisfy her. Halso preached on with his story of how only God could satisfy her. I was doomed. My secret solution for getting her satisfied was for her to kiss a girl of her liking.

The Thursday before our final game of the season, Coach told us we could go home early. Nobody on the team wanted to go, so we stayed and played until it got dark. Most of the guys had parents who came and got them as soon as the sun dropped. I decided to catch the last bus downtown. It was full of Mexican maids returning to their Juarez houses. At the end of the line, they would walk across the border into another country. Some of their children were underneath the bridge that crosses our dry river. Sons and daughters of these hardworking women held cones made of newspaper and waited for the drunk tourists to toss coins into them. After two or three more bus rides they finally crossed the border, and most of the maids would arrive home. Having left their shacks at five-thirty in the morning, they were fortunate if they got back home before ten in the evening.

The bus was crowded and the maids ordered me to wiggle in. Three voices in unison informed the rest of the crowd that I was la Doña Kika's nieto. I hated how the maids from Juarez chewed their gum. The thought of being covered with their sweaty bodies while they clacked Chiclets in uniform contempt for humanity made me uneasy about boarding the bus. The impatient bus driver demanded that I make a decision. I answered that my cousin was on his way to pick me up and the driver squished the door shut.

At the four corners, where I sat alone, stood a church, a Catholic school, a playground used for baseball practice by the best Little League team in the city, and a house with a small entrance through a peeling green archway. A three-story house with wild lights, stories of brujas who read men's souls with poison cure, and public women who charged for the secrets of sin. Rumors of the house included stories of small children who had been stolen and offered to el diablo as sacrifices. Of course, the children most exposed to being kidnapped were those who did not attend Mass on holy days of obligation.

The corner got darker as I watched black diesel smoke pour into the purple night. I heard the clacking of impossible dreams bounding down the street as drops of my tears rolled and sizzled into the hot exhaust. A caravan from hunger returning to its country. I continued to sit on the bus bench, quietly punching the pocket of my mitt to keep it in shape. Although I was a sissy at the plate during real games, I could catch the ball anytime, anywhere, all night long. The day the Chicago Cubs came to play the El Paso Sun Kings, the entire Little League ditched school and I got to ask the great Ernie Banks a question. He answered, advising the crowd to keep their leather in shape. He added something my coach had always said, "Those who don't hit well are just as important to the rest of the team as the big guns. A team accepts everyone's weaknesses and plays together with their strengths." I listened when Ernie Banks had said to keep the pocket of my mitt trained.

I continued training my mitt. The names of the other Cubs escaped me. I couldn't remember Luis Aparicio at short stop. *No. Luis is a White Sox player. No.* When I was afraid, I tried to remember the baseball players and their teams. *Where does Ernie play? What team is he on? The mad house on the corner, bulging into light, becomes a ship in the night sailing off the coast of Chile. All things I know escape me. I am small and alone. Hidden in the darkness. Across the street, lights bathe me in a mystery of luxury. The top floors of the house glow in yellows and dim pinks and brightened windows explode on my skin. There is no punishment. I see creamy skin pausing against reflections of gentle smiles. A party for shadows.*

I heard the purchased breathing of women whose smiles and legs and arms and breasts I had seen in magazines that my older cousins keep hidden in their bedrooms.

He tells me to wait here. He is going inside to get her. I ask if he has a ball and, sure enough, he gives me one to help me train my mitt. I say I will wait quietly. He insists that I will be safe here and not to worry about the dark. Train my glove and wait while he goes to get mommy. I believe him and tell him so. He has never lied before. So, I believe. "Oh, and we have never talked together this much. I like the ball you gave me. Is it new?" He promises to play catch when he returns.

"O.K." I sit still and train my mitt. A big dog appears. It is huge with red, green, and brown fur. Through grey eyes, I know he is a boy dog. He stands across from me as if here to protect me. He is not a Nazi dog. I continue training my mitt. Punching leather in panic. A quiet breath. A silent watch. A beast in wild lights lighted by storm candles. The quieter I get, the madder the dog becomes. Magic flames get too hot and scary. The man who left me here comes back and holds me. "Daddy, you're back. Did you get mommy? Daddy?"

He holds me and I grab him tightly. "Hijo, wake up. Wake up, son."

His whiskers scratch against my Little League face. I do not want to let go of him. He feels brave. "Daddy, did you get mommy?"

His voice amplified. He dropped me onto the front seat of a car, "Hijo, what are you doing here? Where do you live, son?"

My fuzzy eyes tried to focus. Patent leather blue on a shiny hat glitter. Splotches of my muddy fingers on his thick, dark neck. I realized that these fine, large, shoulders were not my daddy's and that we had met during unknown moments of my sleep. He stopped when he saw my slumped frame on the bus stop bench. He wondered if I was wounded or dead. I laughed and said, "My coach thinks I am dead at the plate." Our time together was less than an hour. We laughed together like old sluggers, remembering all the bad pitches we'd swung at.

I have forgotten his name, but I remember that he was a gift. I remember, too, all the presents my father promised and never sent. That stranger in shiny shoes with a rough face and a fat, round belly above skinny legs anchored in me the belief that crossing the river was my right. I remember more of him than I do of my father.

IV

The

Bird

Cage

Was

Not

Perfect

My abuela said, "This house is so big and yellow that all the canaries in the world think they were born here." Abuela would laugh and toss the niños outside when she had had enough of our chirping. "I spend the majority of my life at the mercado." When the first floor of the grand old canary cage got too boisterous with puny little kids, she would send us out. "I only get to be home for such a short time. You niños need to stay out of here so I can get some rest. Maybe I should just take my bed and sofa to the mercado and live there. How would you like that?"

My prima Red, my best cousin, would always respond, "Bueno, Nana, but leave us the tele."

Granny would laugh with Red and then tell us, "Now, go get some fresh air. You know how far to go. And I don't want any trouble from anybody. Buzzy, you too, go outside. Why do you never want to be outside? At the mercado when I have something for you to do you are always outside. What is that you tell me after I find you? When I tell you to go back to work. 'Nana. I was just outside thinking.' Well, hijo go outside now and do some more of that thinking."

The house was a very simple pale yellow with white trim. It was tremendous. There were five levels. Even though it was really a three-story house, cousin Red and I counted the attic and Tío Martín's basement "bachelor pad" as two separate levels. Red snuck into his basement more than I did. I was still playing Little League baseball when she first moved into abuelita's house. Red and I were in the attic when she first told me about a fake lock on one of the back windows of the basement. Red said she had learned all about writing from tío. And that he let her sneak into his basement. He told Red that if she saw him come home alone and if she felt like visiting him late at night, that she could sneak in through the rear window to visit him. For a long time in her young life, she felt like going there a lot. "I got tired of him always being busy with some new vieja de Juarez. Tío needs to stay on this side for a while. But Buzzy, he has so many books in there. Everything you would ever want to read. It's better than the library because if you sneak in when tío is at work, nobody will ever bother you. There is no phone down there and he keeps the front door locked like it is Fort Knox."

La Red and I were the only ones in the family who ever went up to the attic. It was the most enchanting room for me. Red said it was the most peaceful room for her. The other cousins didn't like to climb up the ladder that led to the entryway. More often than not there would be pigeons on the roof in front of the window. Whenever I climbed up there, either alone or with Red, the birds just seemed to be waiting for people to tell them to leave. They would hustle off the roof with a pissed-off coo, but they respected us enough to stay away until we had climbed back downstairs. The dirty birds, la Red, and I shared a rare space in that attic. It was one of those doors that so many on this planet search for. It was an unlocked entryway toward heaven.

The attic was warm and the screens on the windows were torn. There were only two large pillows in the attic. Cushions for the lethargy . . . a silent cloud on top of the roof. Above the street, above the spectacular laughter of Don Martín, abuelita, Tío Martín. Above the flame that left me alone, above the desire that drove Red into madness, raging at all men, all women, all things on earth that destroyed love, above the schoolchild first being sent away from school for not knowing how to read in English, above the joy of first kissing Yolanda, first sleeping between the earth of a sleeping woman, above the empty day when my mother left me, above the empty day when my father left me, above the empty day when my sisters were taken from me, queerly staying in the attic, too sick and stupid to come downstairs and say goodbye, too mad that they were going with her and I was being left behind, too little and too belligerent to know that we would never again see each other.

Tío Martín's room was the entire basement. When he decided to come back and live there, he blocked off the inside entrance to the basement. This left only one entrance, which was down the outside stairway. It led to his front door. Cousin Red, our wildest cousin, the writer, the carpenter who smoked mota, took me to the back of the house. The 3:33 Southern Pacific rumbled behind us. She said we would have to wait until it passed by. "You can't break in when the passenger trains pass by. Tío said he knows all the SP conductors and they watch his place. If they see someone trying to get in through this window, they'll pull the emergency brakes and stop the train." She showed me the fake lock on the tiny window. I had always noticed the locks on all three of the back windows and just kept away.

"Red, the only times I've been in his room, there are always two or three other cousins yelling at uncle to tell us more stories. I have wanted to sneak back into his room and be alone there for a long time. I feel like there is something in that room I need to find."

"Buzzy, when you grow out of your sissy-looking cuerpo de mujer, your new body probably won't be able to squeeze through this window. So watch how I turn this lock and remember exactly how to put it back on." My regular visits to uncle's basement began as I crawled through the window with the phony lock.

Red continued to explain, "One time, I was down here late in the day when I should've been in school and tío was out somewhere. I read his books and drunk some of his vino. Then I stole a bunch of his mota. I smoked too much and got really high and when I went back out the window, I forgot which direction he told me to have that little arrow pointing."

"What arrow?"

"Look at this lock. See that tiny little arrow? He scratched it in with something so that it always points down when it's locked. Sometimes he comes home and looks at his back windows before going downstairs. If the arrow isn't pointing down, he knows somebody is up to something. That is how he knew I stole his mota."

I still didn't understand how uncle knew it was La Red who stole his mota. "Well yeah, Red, big deal, how could he prove you from a burglar?"

Red told me that Uncle Martín made her promise him she would never steal any of his things or he would create a new secret lock and he would not tell her about it. She promised. He said if she didn't keep her promise, he would spank her, too. Red laughed the most curious laugh I had ever heard from her. It was full of something different. Somewhere, there was a secret within her that she was just finding. Many years later, the recollection of that single laugh would touch me in soft places when I had bad dreams. Red had laughed a laugh I would always want to know more about. We stared at each other as if we knew why. Then we climbed downstairs and ran into the shouts of other cousins who were looking for us to come outside and play with them.

Whenever Rosemary wore her carpenter's overalls she insisted on being called "Red." I stuck to calling her La Red all the time. We were walking across the street to buy some ice cream and I continued to ask her about sneaking down into the basement. She got nervous and told me, "Buzzy, quieto. Let's not talk about me and uncle anymore. Tío installed the phony lock because he needs a safety latch in case he loses his keys or something. He told me not to tell anybody. Nobody. After he caught me, I knew that I always had to pay attention to the arrow. I knew that if uncle came home with some vieja, I still had enough time to jump out of the basement and attach the fake lock because their voices would be so loud and full of wanting to get inside, it would take him forever to unlock that ugly front door. Sometimes, when he comes home alone, I wait for him to unlock his door. Then I surprise him. It is okay with him as long as Nana Kika doesn't know I'm staying up so late."

The yellow canary cage in a desert city so full of hungry birds. Cousin Red was the hungriest bird I knew.

V

A
Carpenter
and
a
Writer

Bertha Espinoza, Red's mother, had one daughter and one son. The oldest, her son Jimmy, moved to San Francisco at age nineteen. Everybody knew he liked to be with other guys. Her daughter, Rosemary, "La Red," said she was going to be two things in life: a carpenter and a writer. She wanted to sell best-selling stories to the magazines and she wanted to be a woman who could build things. She was also the brightest and prettiest red-haired, green-eyed girl to ever live in West Tejas. When Jimmy lived at home, he was La Red's fashion coordinator.

The marriage of Bertha and Arturo had been good for many years. Then, as suddenly as a bicycle thief on a kid's birthday, Arturo Espinoza, my dad's cousin from abuelito's brother, decided to leave El Paso. He left the desert with a twenty-one-year-old blondie from the west side of town. Arturo and Bertha had lived in a matrimony that the Catholic Church would have sanctified. Arturo was an engineer for the Southern Pacific. La Red's mother had worked at Texas Western College for ten years. Bertha was head secretary for the president of the college. If you wanted to know anything about the president, much less talk to him, you had to go through Bertha first.

They lived in a small brick house with a small lawn and two large trees. Because Arturo was on the rails so much, he never did anything around the house. Many functions at the college needed Bertha's time and effort. Little Red and little Jimmy saw more of the maids at home than they did their parents. It was fine. La Red was trapped in a cloud that did not allow her to see anything except the small footsteps to school, the jumping and skipping, the screaming on the playground, running and chasing other kids, silently sleeping through boring classes with boring teachers, walking home on the shade side of the street when the sun was too fuerte, and watching little Jimmy put on Bertha's clothes as they pretend to be sisters. La Red insisting she can build things and Jimmy claiming he can see things, and both of them laughing, laughing, and not once thinking that it could end.

When Red realized her life would never be the same, I was spending Saturday night with Rosemary and Jimmy. The phone rang right after midnight. Bertha held the phone to her breast for a long time after she finished her conversation. We had not gone to sleep and we watched her hang up. It looked like she was going to vomit and then she started to take deep, hard breaths. After a million deep sighs, Bertha softly reported that their dad was not coming home.

"Did the train break again, mommy?" Jimmy always worried that the trains would break.

Bertha wanted to say yes, but she didn't.

Rosemary paid attention to something that seemed to be wrapping sheets of wire around her mom. "¿Qué, mom? What is wrong?"

Bertha stood up and walked into the kitchen. She ran to the kitchen door and opened it. "¡Cabrón! ¡Hijo de puta! And he always promised me that he would put up a screen door so we could have a breeze through this house. Ten years we've lived in this house and the only door without a screen is this one. Maybe he'll bring her over and she can help him hang it. I'd like to hang the both of them." Bertha slammed the door so hard that we came running into the room.

Red put her arms around her mother and promised to learn carpentry so that someday she could make her mommy a screen door. Bertha wailed in a tone that none of us had heard since the death of our dear cousin Gloria.

Jimmy asked if he could see where his daddy is on the map and Bertha fell to the floor. He asked, "Mom, is dad dead?"

It took a few moments for Bertha to answer. She told her son that his father should be dead. "No one deserves to be treated the way he treated me."

Two weeks after the divorce was granted, Arturo moved to Tucson with the blondie. Jimmy left for San Francisco. Bertha put the house up for rent and dropped La Red off at Nana Kika's. Bertha told abuelita that she needed some time to find herself. It took her four years to return to El Paso.

By the time Bertha moved back into her old house, Red and I were constantly together. We would go visit Bertha frequently so that we could spend the night away from the endless traffic of family at Nana Kika's. Red was uncertain about moving back in with her mom full time.

Red framed the screen door. She was planning to hang it before morning to surprise her mommy, but the hinges were too big for the door. "Mom. Remember that day when you were so scared and you screamed in the kitchen that your Arturo had never put up a screen door in this room? Remember how I told you that I would learn how to do it and that someday, I would hang it? Mommy, today is your day."

"Sí, Rosie, pero mi'ja can you try not to be so mean?"

"Don't blame me. Blame it on that stupid husband of yours who drives trains." La Red picked up the too-large hinges and left the house. She drove an old Chevy flatbed with a broken fence that Tío Martín gave her because she was such a good apprentice. As she turned the truck onto the highway, Red fired up a joint. She knew there's nothing finer than wearing her carpenter's overalls and working on a project. The road was slow, so she thought about the hinges. There was no time to gather desire in her heart because she was working. And working, for her, always kept the boys away. She was fine with that, too, because being a carpenter, she knew how to use her hands.

Red looked at her just hammered thumb and yelled to God about his mother. She also called her a whore. "Puta, madre de dios." La Red is lefthanded, so her brown right thumb was bleeding and swelling.

"¡Rosie, no diga eso!" Rosemary's mom is the only one who was ever allowed to call this seventeen-year-old carpenter anything other than Rosemary.

"Fuck!"

"¡Rosie!"

"Fuck!"

"Mi'ja, go buy a dress or something and give up on that stupid door. Mauro said he would put it up next week. He has the right tools, too."

Red always called me her "primo Buzzy-ayúdame con esto-Fixit." Never Digit. When she was really high on mota, she peacefully revealed to me that she would marry me if I wasn't such a sissy . . . and then she laughed, remembering the time I struck out with the bases loaded and two outs in the bottom of the seventh inning when the panadero's team was trying to get past that fucking Lubbock team. "Of course I struck out, I didn't have my glasses on."

"O, Buzzy, everybody knows you're a sissy at the plate on game days. Yo quíero saber why you are. And just when it's time to win."

Red scratched herself in front of me and I felt like her sister. We settled into each other's eyes and streaked into the open desert with our blood hot and our lips soft and our legs heavy with the weight we carry. Our feet were toughened by splinters from thousands of thorns, thorns that gave themselves to protect the rose. For the soft belligerence of beauty, la little Red and I embraced in envelopes that would one day be mailed across an island . . . the island of dreams, dreams of peace, dreams of little girls first touching their softness, dreams of little fine dreamers surviving the first leathery mad howl of a mother cornered by a man. The first violent howl of a little girl being grabbed by a man with diesel, oil, beer, smoke everywhere on his body, with the small girl and her small fingers having to touch his horrible thing, with the smile from the satisfied, not knowing that the lost one is not the child. Then, with the smile of survivors, La Red and I danced in the blue sad light of her bedroom . . . a room filled with soft flowers and soft eyes of the toughest girl in the barrio.

VI

Lottery

Winners

By the time I was about to get drafted into the Army, Red and Wanna became lovers. I looked at my watch before opening the door to a tornado of two women in love. I had just estimated there were four days, four hours, and four minutes left to my life as a civilian. I told Rosemary and Wanna. "Four, four, four."

I think they both answered at the same time. "Qué chingaos es eso? Four, four, four. What the fuck?"

Red and Aunt Wanna stopped moving furniture. Both of them fell down onto the couch. Red started right away about her blond Aunt Wanna. Her aunt was wearing a dark green mini-skirt and a white top that revealed the destination of her nipples. Her wavy hair was pointing all across Tejas. Silently, as Red rambled, Wanna spread her legs apart.

"Buzzy, I don't know what your numbers mean right now, but do you know what my twatty tía just told me? She told me to stop using her. Buzzy, help me. Jee, fuck." Rosemary's spaghetti-strap, black dress was torn. Her top lip was swollen. Her left hand was scratched and the blood had dried across her knuckles. Aunt Wanna had harsh, bloodied fingers. Red and her first woman lover had just finished a lover's quarrel.

"I was counting the time I have left before I go into the army. I know you don't like to hear that I am really going. You think you guys will still be together when I get out? All you do these days is fight." The day was filled with numbers. I counted how many men I had been with. How many women. I had been with more men than girls. Girls always wanted to be my friend. Men wanted me cause I didn't care.

Red was in the process of moving in with Wanna but most of her furniture had been sitting on the outside porch for two days. Red wanted to move it inside but Aunt Wanna wanted her to wait until the Salvation Army came to haul away some of the old furniture from inside the house. When the slugging stopped, La Red had reached for the phone and pleaded with me to come over.

I didn't run to their house because that day I walked with a lonely shadow. When I was lonely I started to count numbers. All my other cousins had mothers and fathers somewhere within reach. I started counting how many girl cousins I had. It was too confusing. How should I count Red? Some of my cousins had brothers and sisters from a new mom or dad who lived in the same house. Or at least the same city, if they had to spend time at Nana Kika's in order to get away from family problems. How many postcards would they get if a parent went out of town? My father sent me many postcards, but none with a return address. In all the years since my mother left, I could count three letters from her. The last one being the most cruel.

I was twelve and playing my last year of Little League. My mother, Isabella, wrote that she and her husband and my sisters would all be there that summer. She did not know exactly when, but she promised. It was the first time I believed one of her promises. That summer, every night, I would stay in the front yard, refusing to go anywhere because I wanted to be outside when they arrived. I wanted her and my sisters to see me first. The summer ended without them. They never came.

Wanna's husband, Arturo's brother, had been dead all of our lives. Red was nine years old when she began to spend most of her time at beautiful Auntie Waawaa's house. Tía would encourage la baby Red to show off, "because it is the fastest way to make a man feel like loving you." She told her.

Wanna wore evening dresses that made the wetness inside her a widely available gift. She had a need to get tied into herself. A desire to attack dignity with a loud howling in the accent of a girl from another country. Young and old soldiers. She called them all "boys." They attacked her language with songs from their hometowns. With their religions. They said their homes were better places than this desert. As they invaded her, she listened to their stories. Still, their special courtyards walled out the pressure of loving. They were just passing through, on their prescribed passage with her for a fun fuck which made them men upon their return home.

Wanna's men behaved like they had been tossed from the arms of mothers whose milk had dried too quickly after they were born. Too many of them told the same story and were so alike that Wanna could no longer distinguish men from boys or tiny from big. Wanna got to know them all as she piously wandered across the military base called Fort Bliss. She had been there long before I was drafted.

One time Red got mad at me and tossed her dirty panties in my face. Wanna and Red had just begun their affair and I was mad because I was feeling left out of La Red's life. I let the panties sit on my face. Then, I chewed and sucked on the crotch. I tasted her blood. We laughed and she helped me finish my make-up. We were like that together. We came with each other many times. It was something to do while we searched for our mates. We promised each other that no one would ever know about us. I was a boy stepping into his sister's dress and we kept our secret in wisdom like the silence of gods. She liked me inside of her and she giggled when I told her to squeeze as many fingers as she could push into me. She said that if I had a cunt, I would be a big whore. And that she would make me into a big, rich, sophisticated one. We did everything together. We licked each other. I took her from behind. She took me from behind. I watched her do things on the toilet. She held me when I peed. I changed her pads when she bled. And we once watched ourselves together in the mirror. She got tired of pleasing me and I got tired of pleasing her, but we stayed together because we were in love.

"Buzzy, when does the mailman come?"

"Whenever he wants to put something in your slot, slut."

We were that way together.

"Buzzy Digit, you stroke my hair like you love me." Red and I were sitting in the attic on New Year's Eve. She was eighteen. A foamy flame thower. A girl that wanted me. A genuis of a girl because I wanted her and she knew that. Always knew that. It would be our last New Year's Eve together. I was going to war. A great gathering was already underway downstairs in Nana Kika's big yellow bird cage. The greatest parade of our time would wind its way in front of our home on Montana Street. Our canary cage was the last house on the right before the procession crossed the railroad tracks. I continued stroking La Red's hair and she started to laugh. "Remember how funny it was last year when the train stopped the parade? You know, the Southern Pacific has never crossed those tracks during the parade."

I stopped touching her and opened the attic window so that we could climb onto the roof. I whispered, "I remember how crazy the crowd got. Those vatos across the street started throwing all their stolen beers at the engine when it stopped in the middle of the street. The band from Bowie High was stuck there and they kept playing their fight song and ducking the splashing beer from the tossed broken bottles. Remember all our uncles going crazy and singing along with their old high school band while they were fighting with the train?"

La Red wrapped her soft hands on her breast and asked me how I knew that the beer had been stolen. "Red, half those guys across the street I knew. Do you remember that guy with the long hair and black hat? Last year, you couldn't miss him . . . he was the only one of the guys who dressed that way."

"Buzzy, you mean that guy that the cops took first? He was wearing Tony Lama's and those tight blue Levi's and his hair was almost down to his neck and his white shirt was unbuttoned and his belly was really pretty and his nipples were gorgeous and brown?"

Red Rosemary and I sat on the roof watching the night prepare itself for the next day. I asked her with a tortured voice, "How did you know his nipples were brown?"

"Well, Buzzy baby, I wanted to suck them."

"So did I Red."

"Buzzy, you're such a queer. If only I could get you to start acting like your cousin Jimmy, then we can keep you out of that fucking army."

Rosemary was with me when I reported for my physical after the papers arrived ordering me into the army at the whim of our Tío Sam. She did not stop talking. She yelled at the room full of sergeants that I was "as joto as the night is dark." Embarrassed by my guardian angel cousin, I sat on an iron bench with my legs crossed and my mind in a race to the everywhere of desire.

"Red, shut up."

"Fuck you, Buzzy. They are not taking you."

"Yeah, but don't be telling everybody about me."

"You *are* a sissy. They can't take you. I won't let them. What are you going to do when it comes to fighting? You don't even know how to use your knuckles. The other day when that stupid punk was trying to rape me, what did you do? Nothing. I hit the fucker on his huevos and kicked his ass out of the house. You, in the meantime, just pranced about like you needed to get fucked in the butt. You are a sissy. You fucking queer. I love you and nobody is taking you away from me."

The examining room was full of men. No one heard our conversation. The military clerks no longer listened to excuses from the draftees.

"Dysiaaiadidcheck . . . whatever the hell your name is, come to the counter."

Rosemary screamed at the men, "You cocksuckers! You can't have this fucking queer."

Sergeants exchanged cigarettes and notes on the "evaders." Not once did they respond to my sweet angel Rosemary. They ignored everything she said. They had heard worse. Yesterday, a mother had walked in with her son and broke a bottle of pulque across his head.

The stitches only delayed his draft by a few hours. The Tejas border was especially kind to volunteers who were needed to fight in southeast Asia. Rosemary was protesting to a room full of machines.

VII

Some

of

Us

Are

Missing

My two sisters were either a memory or a dream. Olivia was a tangerine. She looked like Elizabeth Taylor in *National Velvet*. She was a sweet mix of good things. Olivia is the oldest child. She always held my hand as we entered the school, which was run like a prison by the nuns of Asilomar. Old, rough women dressed in the blackness of Halloween. Asilomar is not by the sea. It is an abandoned monastery on the east side of El Paso near a chicken farm and two factories. A man-made lake nearby gives the workers from the factories priority boating privileges. My uncles used to laugh at this because the lake was so full of weeds that even if you owned a motor boat, it would get stuck and tangled in wet catfish weeds. And if you caught a fish, no one would eat it because of the smell. Not the fish smell. The smell of a sweating gavacho.

Leticia was the tough one. She was my defender once we entered the gates of this children's hell. She was like a sturdy plough horse. Leticia chewed bubble gum and spit all day long. Nana Kika always said that I remembered Olivia and Leticia more through my dreams than she could through her memory. I asked abuelita if she remembered Tío Martín coming to pick up all the kids in his truck during an emergency when the stupid Asilomar got closed down by some court order. Abuelita scratched her head. She remembered Uncle Martín taking us there every morning, but she said Asilomar was never shut down. I tell her my dreams wish it had been.

The water in the center fountain was brown and smelled like a raw sewer. The older kids threatened to throw me in unless I gave them my lunch. This happened daily. And daily, Leticia came running from her circle of toughs, chasing the thieves away and threatening to slice off their hanging huevos.

My sisters never hit me. They liked me and I liked them. Leticia said I was too skinny to be a boy and that I would probably be a sissy. Olivia told her to shut up. Olivia was a very proper lady. She already wore lipstick, stood straight, and wore ironed dresses.

The dreams stopped at Asilomar. The road to Asilomar was always gray. Even when the sun was shining on El Paso and on top of Nana Kika's house and all over the West Tejas tierra of old rocks and old drinkers and old runaway dreamers, the road to our nursery was always gray. Grandchildren between the ages of five and ten were convinced they had been sentenced to this chamber pot of nuns. We were certain the sisters who controlled this place were secret fugitives from a hardass back country controlled by Hitler. The nuns had given in to the other side. They did not know my god.

Uncle Martín blew the horn from delivery truck No. 1 of the Panadería Don Martín while he yelled to me and all my cousins that "the last one in would not get to lick frosting from the early leftovers." I didn't know about him. No one was ever the last one in. Usually, eight or ten of us were in the back of the bread van bouncing, giggling, spitting, farting, screaming, pulling something of someone else's, and generally making the morning as loud as possible. This, after having just barely opened our eyes, crying that we were too dead to move. Most mornings, once we stopped bouncing and wiggling, Tío Martín would tell us a story of his adventures of the previous night.

"A baker's day begins at midnight." A baker, like our Tío Martín, began his day during the hours before midnight. Depending on how far apart his current women lived, he could be out on the street as early as six in the evening. Abuelo left behind a legacy for his sons that said, "Bread must always be fresh and work must begin at exactly noon with an upside down moon." Tío Martín, despite his wild ways and beyond his rum, was always on time at the bakery. He was the jefe now that his dad was gone. But he had not learned as much about the ways of women as he had about what happens to the seeds that are planted in women. Muchos sobrinos y sobrinas. Lots of lost children.

In the early sparkle of the supernatural morning on our way to an eerie border town hell, our hungover uncle filled the van with the loudest, stinkiest fart and then told us his story. It was always about a woman for whom he had done everything. Even gave her a job at the panadería.

"You try to be her friend but she doesn't want a friend. She says she already has too many friends. She wants more than just a friendly night out. She wants to see baby tears on her breasts . . . I tell her I can cry but she says I be already too old and feo . . . but I tell her I'm old, and not too ugly—to pretend baby stuff." By then, the van became a rolling steel laugh box.

Leticia grasped her breasts and asks, "How big are her chi chi's?"

Uncle Martín suddenly got proper, responding priest-like. "Ay, mi'ja, what kinda question is that?"

I asked him about the color of her eyes and he told me that there is much more to a woman than the color of her eyes. I said I don't think so and he told me that my mother's eyes were the prettiest eyes he has ever seen. So many times he wished that my dad had . . . then tío trailed off into an adult silence.

Isabella, my mother, held me against her breast. She was saying goodbye. "Adios, mi'jo." I changed my smile to match hers. We were mirrors. I was on top of her. She kept her left hand in my hair. Isabella's right hand was on my buttocks. My face breathing on her breast. "My baby, I have to become his sister."

"Isabella, I will be your brother if you take me with."

"He only wants girls, mi'jo. I can pass as his oldest daughter and Olivia and Leticia can pass as my baby sisters."

"Mommy." I cried and she let me suckle her breast again. I was six years old on my way to being left behind at Nana Kika'a house. It was my birthday. Isabella gave me a blue Timex watch. She put her fingers around her nipple and continued to stroke my hair. I did not want to stop crying.

"Baby. Mi'jo. Honey. Listen to me baby, I will come back to get you. Just let me be his girl for a little while and then I know he will let you come with us. He is a good man."

I don't remember when I stopped crying.

"So much memory will destroy us . . . join me in my prayers. Join me in my prayers. I am the last woman who will ever love you. I am drowning but you cannot do anything about it. Remember Gloria? I drown like her. Take my hand mi'jo, and hold me against your heart. I am the last woman who will ever love you this way. It is cold right now. It is so cold. Sit on my lap. I know you think you're too big, but, angel mi'jo, you will never be too big to sit between my legs. I changed your diapers. I was so young. I am still so young. He wants me to be his sister. The girls will be my sisters, but I can't make you my brother. I can't make you anything . . . you are my baby boy. I will dream of you.

Sand on your fingers. The opposite eyes of mine. The tender small laughter. Boy of mine. I don't know how to ask you to forgive me. I can only say goodbye. I can only say . . . ."

I don't remember when I stopped crying.

VIII

Bienvenidos
to
the
South

The preparations for the party started when Ricky Roy and Tío Martín got into a huge tearful discussion about Gina, pobrecita, and her need to feel accepted by todos en la familia. Poor Gina. She did not feel welcome. Our big Biloxi blonde wanted Nana Kika to make her feel like she belonged. It was a Wednesday morning. My oldest boy cousin and my oldest uncle were drinking beer, sitting in abuelita's kitchen. On the days when I knew the divorced Mrs. Triana was home, I would peek into her bathroom window from six-thirty to seven.

My oldest boy cousin, the twenty-five-year-old Ricky Roy Inclava, offered his house as a place "to fly away from the canary cage whenever you want to." It was at the end of my young baseball career. We were driving back from Odessa after having lost in the regional. "Look, you need to come over to our house more often. And when you want to, if there is work to do, Gina will tell you what to do. You can make some extra money."

The water in Nana Kika's bottle contained truth. Ricky Roy despised my attitude. My laughter bothered him. I was twelve years old and drunk for the first time. He was not laughing as he picked me up from the garage floor and promised me that I am going straight toward el diablo. Then I puked on his shiny, police-trainee shoes.

My big-shot cousin was a high school cheer-leader's dream. But to me, he was a mutt. After my first encounter with the gavacho dog, I yelled at Ricky Roy, "Doggie boy Roy is the same as Leroy." The only Leroy we knew was the Nazi, Leroy Harvay. Ricky chased me, threatening to remove the most important of my young organs. Nana Kika saved me by yelling at him to leave me alone as I continued running and laughing that refrain, "Doggie boy Roy is the same as Leroy."

Ricky Roy returned from the Air Force after having survived the Nam by being stationed for four years at Keesler Air Force Base in Biloxi, Mississippi. But he did not survive the demands of a trio from the South. He married a big, loud, pink woman from Biloxi who al-ready had two daughters. Gina Halinger said she was twenty-nine and continued to say this for several years after I first met her. I figured she must have been saying it for a few years before she arrived in El Paso.

Gina was a big opposition of a girl. She had pretty blue-green eyes like a mountain lake before winter. Yet she looked like a bully. The erotic pain of giving had ab-sorbed her. Gina was the leather sting of a strap against the inside of a thigh. She wore brassy earrings and giant bright rings on her fingers. Her southern breasts were a tremendous escape from the oppression of segregation. She wore lips in colors sworn to secret, futile kisses. She had the look of forever as if she had just been saved from a bottomless pit of gloom. Her painted toes had curled over the fresh cut roses of many a dreamy lover. Gina's shoes never had less than four inches of heel.

I am inside their house for another of my frequent intrusions. No one is home. The two girls, Charmaine and Heather, are in school and Gina is at a baking class. I walk into her closet and begin an aroma test of her soiled undies. I start with a skin test of her married materials on my crotch when the bedroom door explodes open and my stupid cousin and his big, horny wife enter. I hide, in fear of my life, in the darkest corner of the closet surrounded by four-inch heels for more than forty-seven minutes. I tell myself that if I survive this burglary, I will keep it secret and take it with me to my grave.

The sweat of their exhausted bodies finally gave way to a joint shower. Once they were both under the gushing water, I bolted, clutching an imprinted pair of my favorite panties. Those that have been worn being filled with a man's orgasms.

My dead cousin Gloria's brother, Ricky Roy, married this woman with the Southern white English accent from Biloxi. Their wedding was held in the rain on the Gulf a week before they came back to Texas. In all his letters he had promised to bring back sweets. I figured it was going to be something better than leche quemada. I did not like her for anything except the leaked-on smell of her panties and the feel of her high heels. She was an interference in my lifetime of mourning for our familia's loss of the seizure-prone Gloria. No one could possibly expect to triumph in a deeper tragedy than mine.

The first story Gina told me was one of how she found her brother dead in a side creek of the Mississippi. His body had oozed in the water for several days. She said it looked like bread that had soaked in milk too long. "If you aren't careful when lifting the body out, it will fall apart." His rescuers wrapped canvas and sheets of plastic around her brother's body before removing it from the muddy stream. He was only twelve years old when someone did things inside his butt, then shot him and tossed his thin body into the river.

Gina's oldest daughter, Charmaine, was turning fifteen and was very much on my right-handed thoughts. Charmaine wanted to be proper. She considered us relatives, so she would not kiss me. She would kiss my buddies, but she would not kiss me because I was her "family." I tried to explain that we were family on paper only, but this did not convince her to kiss me. Even after I rescued her from countless cheap wine highs on the hillsides of our brown, desolate, suicidal desert town, she refused to kiss me and begged me to stay the way I was. I thought stealing panties from her mama's closet was a terrible way to stay, but since she insisted so kindly, I decided hers would be next.

Their house was the landing site of imported women. The other import, young ten-year-old Heather, immediately labeled me a pagan. When she arrived in El

Paso, she believed in stuff like the Resurrection and a responsibility to the meek through guidance toward salvation. She also feared that savages like me and my friends might someday rule the world. This poor, pink, prepubescent Biloxi brat with no straight teeth and wild grass for hair and big ears and wrinkled, freckled hands and big areolas on tiny tits, became a major pusher of brown Mexican heroin in West Tejas. If she had anything, she had drive.

A few years later, when I was stationed at Fort Bliss, before being shipped overseas, Heather was my best source for dope.

At seven-thirty in the morning, I finished my paper route and ran to la tolstoyería to watch the girls. A little house run by red skinny people dressed in the clothes worn by slaves in those bible movies. Nana Kika insisted it was a whorehouse but I kept telling her that those people were believers in loving for free. "Niño, qué es love free?" I never had an answer for her. But I told her that if she wanted to come with me to their house they would explain everything to her, too.

"Nana, they call themselves beatniks and they talk about how children do not belong to their parents, wives do not belong to their husbands, congregations do not belong to their preachers, workers do not belong to the owners." The guys who did all the talking looked like gladiators and had beautiful, big, thick-lipped women hanging around them. All these fine girls looked like they wanted to be somebody's mother. I always dreamed that two or three of them were mine and that I was their shared son.

Nana Kika called it "la tolstoyería" because she never knew who owned the house and who owned the souls. "That ruso, Tolstoy, tried to do the same thing in Mejico . . . cabrón, hijo de puta. . . ." She cautioned me that hanging around this place could give me the most confusing dreams of my young life. "They talk about war as if they know about it, mi'jo. Mi'jo, yo te quiero. I cannot begin to tell you about the razor's edge on us. We survive a thousand wars every day of our life." Señora Kika Soldano ignored my vague response and continued, "No one in there has lost a son to war. I lost *two!* I have more sons. I have more daughters. I have more life. But I *do not have* my two sons! I *do not have* my two sons. I *do not have* my two sons." The only time abuelita ever cried was when she talked of the war and of her lost boys.

I would finish my paper route at the beatnik house. The "wild Tolstoys" were never asleep at five in morning. I could always count on somebody to be laughing. And the girls in that house were so naked. Not that they had their clothes off—it was a part of belonging to the tolstoyería that made the women look naked. I would hand deliver the morning newspaper to that house because someone would be waiting on the porch for my arrival and they would invite me inside. The house had the same smell of Uncle Martín's parked car at a party . . . weeds burning. I would get a daily lecture from a guy or from one of those tremendous women, and I would walk away laughing at how they delivered their speeches to me. It was as if they were trying to save me from something. "Little brother, love should always be free. And the best mota coming into this country right now is from your raza's old country."

Then I went to Mrs. Triana's house to make my appearance outside her bathroom window. She had two morning routines. If her boyfriend's car was in the driveway, she ran through her bathroom functions as if all of time was coming to an end. Then the boyfriend would stumble in, spoiling my fantasy. Ugly man. When there was no car in the driveway and she was alone, I could count on her being lazy, slow, and lovely while sitting on her toilet. She would wipe her crotch, then move her flushed naked buttocks into the middle of my dreams. Watching her study the image of herself in the mirror I thought it was what an angel would do, if it could see its own face. Each morning after I watched her, I floated home with her inside of me.

Uncle Martín watched me walk in the door. He laughed, "Buzzy, you weren't peeking inside anybody's windows were you?"

"No, tío. Not just anyone. Only the redhead."

"Oye, hijo, is she really red down there?"

"I don't know, uncle. You'll have to look for yourself."

Ricky interrupted our fun with his long sad face and ordered me to go to bed. Then he continued talking with Uncle Martín. Ricky Roy and tío had been out all night because Ricky had had a big fight with his wife, left his house, and went to the bakery just as the bread was being baked. The two of them then went to Juarez in Uncle Martín's MG.

Ricky thought that I had gone to bed, but I stood in the hallway. His voice was slow with the dust from a hard night. "Listen, uncle, I feel so sad for her. Gina says Nana Kika won't talk to her whenever they are alone together. Gina knows abuelita understands English, so why won't Nana Kika talk to her en inglés?" Ricky swallowed his beer.

"Mi'jo, your abuelita loves everyone in her familia. Even new additions. Remember that vieja? Christina. You know, the widow you kids used to call, 'wicked witch of the southwest.' Bueno, pues, Cristina and I were going to get married. I was crazy for this woman, who no one else liked. My jefita, your granny, never interfered. She guided me out of that pendejada, out of being such a fool, with one of her crooked threats. And you know how she did it?"

Ricky was crying. "Did what?"

"Do you know how she got me to leave that woman? No? Bueno. Well, Nana Kika caught me with Don Martín's favorite niece, Angelita. She was the first one in his family to go to college. In fact, that old panadero was paying for her school. Don Martín swore her to secrecy because he was afraid someone else in his familia might make it into college and he would have to pay for them, too. But Angelita told me everything. It is a funny thing with virgins. The most crazy thing about them is that they will never tell you about their past. No matter how much they fall in love with you. All you hear about is their secret future. A man can never know how virginal a virgin is. But he knows how good she will be with other men. A virgin was never meant to stay with the first man. Little Angelita was the first one to tell me about her bald round uncle and mi madre getting together. Angelita even knew where they did it. Still, the fat fucker gets my respect. So when your Nana Kika walked in on me and the baker's no-longer-virgin niece, she stood still and straight and said, 'When the day comes that you decide to settle with just one woman, that will be the day I start talking in English.'"

Ricky Roy sounded like he was entering a seminary. "But, uncle, you have been married so many times, I lost count. What? Is it two or three?"

"Hijo, it doesn't matter how many times I've been married. I have never stopped believing in love. I just don't know who to stay in love with."

Nana Kika saw me in the hallway and quietly glided delicate, cold, skinny fingers across the back of my neck. I jumped and screamed like I was trying to leap across the copper canyon. Uncle Martín and Ricky Roy laughed so hard that Nana Kika told them to stop or they would wake every dead dog within a hundred miles. She ordered me to bed. Her laughter came from the belly of a giant.

Uncle talked to his mother like she was a business

partner. "So mama, diga me, qué mujer en esta familia tiene ansia por la felicidad? What makes a woman happy?"

"Hijo, with the things my girls have to look forward to in their lives with men, how can any of our women be too anxious for married happiness?"

Tío Martín was not too smart this morning.

Nana Kika walked up to him, pulled his ear, and told him to go to bed before she herself showed him exactly what it was that made women happy.

My uncle would not stop arguing with someone he would never win an argument with. "Mama, the women I know just want to get it."

"Quieto, niñoso, they only want to pull your huevos. Hard and mean. And you, being the son of my first old panadero, every floja around here wants to be your girl so she can see some of Don Pablo's money. And pues, tu, digame, how can I be happy when I am widowed from the biggest baker in town and now soltera, but very friendly with the biggest tortillero in town? Nothing but the kitchen for me.

Her son, the first Martín in her life, asked, "Y, qué pues con eso? I don't care if somebody wants me for my money if all I want them for is their body."

"Hijo, ya basta. Duérmate." Nana Kika ordered her oldest son to bed.

Watching Nana Kika in the kitchen in the morning was like watching the sun spill heat onto cold, small flowers. Suddenly the room was warm and coffee was being poured. Huevos con chorizo, carne asada from last night, tortillas, and frijoles refritos were served by a woman listening to two men crying about the impossibilities of women.

Tío Martín got up from the table the same way I did when the house was crowded con familia and granny ordered all the pinguinos, us little piggies, to get out of the way of the adults. Uncle moved like a man accused of murder, head to the ground, shoulders rounded and in trouble, feet so heavy—a man so wrong as to help himself immediately with praise for something religious. "Mama, que Dios te bendiga." He asked God to bless his mother.

Ricky Roy bolted upright and smiled at my favorite uncle. "Tío, nana never needs any of us to bless her."

"Rickie, ya vete a tu casa." La Sra. Soldano was firm and in charge. "Go home."

Ricky bolted and was gone in the flash of sunshine on broken glass.

More often than not, after finishing my paper route, I fell asleep before getting ready for school. My granny didn't get mean, sometimes she woke me with her favorite imitations of birds. Other times she sang old songs. Whenever she awakened me, I noticed a certain happiness, one that is restricted and found only in the soul of lost angels. But that day, with newsprint and the satisfaction of having watched Mrs. Triana's bathroom habits all over my fingers, I was startled when granny woke me. She was talking to me in English.

Abuelita was practicing speaking her new language for the party. She was spooky with her, Tejana dialect, "Wake up, niño. Escuela, school, it almost ready, mi'jo."

I screamed.

"Quieto, niño, qué te pasa?" Skinny, white-haired granny flew a gypsy smile across my face. "Quiet, boy. What's wrong with you?"

"Abuelita, I didn't know who you were. What did you just say?"

"Nada, hijo. Nothing." She was both a bug and a ghost, hysterically biting me with her grin.

"O.K."

When I came home from school, big Gina and her southern girls were in the house. Whenever Gina wanted to bake, she would come over to use the big oven installed many years ago by my great and dead grandfather. The baker left behind almost a complete bakery inside the yellow bird cage. Gina was baking some kind of bread I'd never heard of and the girls were both scrambling around the house. Tío Martín told Gina that the family was planning a huge celebration in her honor. Upon hearing that a party was to be given for her, Gina's smile crossed the desert like rain. I began to feel miserable and didn't know why. I didn't want to believe it. After that day in her closet, whenever I saw Mississippi Gina, her smell became the gray beginning of life for me. It was a period of joy so absolute as to remain forever. The breath of yesterday spilled onto her thighs with the excrement of the moon. I wanted her to push my face into her crotch. I wanted her to show me how to kiss. I wanted her to teach me how to love a woman. I wanted her to be close to me. Something beyond a dream. I wanted her to lift my body up and bring me to the river of life. I wanted her to surrender her mothering to a little boy. To forget her own girls. I wanted her to kiss me and let me kiss her back with soft boyhood moans. I never wanted to be around her.

Gina survived my fantasies because she was not interested in me. I knew from the time she walked in on me when I was in the bathtub. I was soaking in the suds, watching my erection surface above the water line, pumping lather and soap on my twelve-year-old penis. When she walked in she only stared at me. Then she said to hurry up because the toilet was waiting for her. The door closed and my little pito collapsed. *Farm girl, Come back and secretly gather my wish between your long fingers and gently stroke me.*

Instead, Gina pounded on the door and told me to close the shower curtain because she couldn't wait any longer. "Damn, Buzzy, I gotta pee so bad my back teeth are floating." I obeyed her command. She stepped into the bathroom and covered the toilet with her Biloxi buttocks and peed. She was too fast for me. I couldn't figure out how to peek at her. I smelled and heard everything. I wanted to watch her so badly, the same way I could watch Mrs. Triana.

Tío Martín talked to his compadres at the Legion Hall and they decided to book the hall for us two weeks from Saturday. The American Legion building was a structure that has seen mayhem, agony, desperation, and many parties. From las bodas de sangre to the high school proms to the official celebration palace for the war veterans, it was the only hall our family ever used for big events. Now it had been scheduled for a welcoming celebration of our new Biloxi girl and her daughters. Ricky Roy was happy. I was nervous. Old man Acosta took control. He said the hall would be fixed up like it was a wedding. Nana Kika and Don Martín negotiated the cost.

When the big day came, it was hot. Nasty desert hot in the middle of summer. For me, that was always the best time of the year. Not only because of baseball, but because all woman smelled of desire in the summer. They stuck themselves full of douches that worked miracles against the air wandering onto the small crevice of their center. I bathed with them and held the nozzle. Deliriously. A small long climb into my lost mother.

A Saturday mass was held before the great ceremony. Cousins I hadn't seen in two years were there. Everyone who had ever worked at the mercado with Nana Kika was there. It felt like everything I had ever read about New York City. Millions of people and endless images. A confusion from the ordinary day. La Red and her new friend quickly hugged me and promised me thousands of smiles if I would steal some mota from Tío Martín's MG. Sure, fine. Girls. My legs are yours to move any direction. Uncle caught me with my hands in his trunk and smiled. "Buzzy, I know this mota is not for you. Who set you up?"

"Tío, I ain't telling."

"Bueno. Don't tell. But the girls don't get any if they can't ask for it themselves."

"How'd you know it was the girls?"

"Hijo, they both got you wrapped around their tiny curls. You don't do nothing for nobody unless it's for them. So just tell them they gotta ask me. Y no digas nada, don't say anything, to you-know-who. If Nana Kika finds out, she can still kick my ass. Tell them to come outside. I'll stay here in the parking lot for a while."

It was a tremendous party. Ricky Roy and all of his stupid police buddies couldn't stop slapping each other around. The women brought my favorite smell with them. It is carried by a woman wanting to be at a party. The uncles from nowhere were now important and talked loudly about their mighty positions in many different companies. Suddenly there were vice-presidents in our family . . . and corporate executives who single-handedly had saved their empire from collapse. One of my lost aunts was now a singer for a band . . . and they were travelling between Silver City and Alamogordo and even Tucson and Phoenix. . . . A vice-president of an oil drilling operation was talking about going to Alaska . . . nobody believed him. I did, and told him that a moose is called an alce. He ignored me.

They banded together with the blandness of lies.

Singers sealed my dreams. The band was eclectic. A tornado at sunrise was all I wanted. But Uncle Martín had told me long ago that El Paso never gets tornados because it is surrounded by mountains. I went outside to the parking lot and listened to him tell his mota-smoking nieces that they should never smoke that stuff with a guy, "unless you are willing to really go crazy . . ."

My great girl cousins asked, in unison, "And you, tío, you are the craziest vato in this entire familia . . . oye and why can't you stay with one slut, O. I mean why can't you stay con una puta no mas. . . ." They laughed big. Two girls who so wildly and quickly became women never stopped treating me like a little sissy boy.

Ricky Roy screamed through a megaphone ordering everyone inside for the special ceremony. Nana Kika welcomed Gina and her daughters in English. My MG uncle and half the vatos in the parking lot missed most of the welcoming ceremony because of their slow walk in to the hall. That night the hall was filled with dresses and dancing shoes, sharp suits, eyes pointing toward the reunion of a moonbeam, wet lips and dry mouths. There was just enough wiggle in my toes to carry a hand on my arm and just enough newness to make me believe I was headed on a trail that led in a straight line to heaven.

Gina, Ricky Roy, the girls, the drunken German priest, and the enormous goodwill and beauty of Nana Kika filled the stage. Ricky spent too much time talking about himself and the Air Force and the South. Gina cried. Gina's girls were oblivious. They must have been hanging around uncle's MG. It had never occurred to me that my grandmother needed to speak in English for anything beyond a simple yes, no, or no entiendo. The priest offered his blessing, but no one was listening because La Señora Kika Soldano was ready to address the crowd. She looked nervous and unprepared. At the mercado, she controlled the crowds. Tonight, she stumbled in words that were not hers. "Hallow, ebb re buddy." It hurt me to listen to her speaking in English.

She went on. "I want to welcome the South to our house." Then she publicly promised to speak more English to Gina and the girls. The high throng of bilingual partygoers gave her loud and lengthy applause. The cheering was so heavy it smashed my feet. Feet that moved me out the door and into the night sky, falling in an entirely new way for me. Never had I seen a sky look so gloomy while being so pretty. Stars were jumping off the hot desert floor of sunset. My favorite pinks were whipping the mountains. I felt lost and alone again for the first time in many years. My feet walked me to the freight yard. I was almost thirteen and ready to hop my first freight out of town.

It felt like I was six years old again and listening to Isabella say things that I did not want to hear. I did not want to hear my abuelita speak to anyone in English. I did not want her to change.

IX

Travelling

with

Men

I hopped the first of many freight trains from El Paso to Los Angeles. Southern Pacific ran a daily passenger train that left for L.A. every morning at 6:45. The one-way fare was $27.45, but I had no money. In the early 1960s, boxcars were free. The first freight I jumped onto contained five men headed for new destinies. No one volunteered a name, so by the time the boxcars were rolling past the smelter town, I had named four of them after my favorite baseball heroes. Ernie Banks was hunched in a corner smoking bright ashes. Luis Aparicio paced back and forth near the door. Jesús Alou stood still, waiting for the next pitch. Juan Marichal was kicking the side of the car. I could not name the last player because he avoided contact with everyone in the boxcar.

A dead body discovered on the side of the rails in Tucson prompted the railyard guards to chase everyone off the train. There was a long delay. The body had been found the day before we arrived. Big men in uniforms with well-fed bellies searched us and kicked us and insisted that we would soon be licking their boots. They said this was a lucky day for us because they decided they did not want their boots to smell like dogs.

Juan picked up a big stick and went after a cop. Ernie grabbed him from behind and scolded him. "The sons-a-bitches will kill us all if we fuck with them." Juan carried the weight of a madman in his eyes. He didn't respond. He was frozen. I listened, petrified, praying for Ernie to keep his hold on Juan. The Chicago Cub became a bear. Ernie held onto the wild beast long enough for us to live. The railyard monsters with badges howled at us to leave their land and their trains.

Ernie told me to follow him. Once we had strayed far enough away from the other travellers, I watched as Ernie rolled a thick cigarette. He handed it to me, saying that if I had never known a strawberry field, I would know one now. Marichal and Alou followed us. They laughed as soon as I took a hit. There was a brief pause in the history of my life and the next sound I heard was a loud scream from Juan telling me to hand him the puta mota. Jesús just stood there, waiting for his next pitch. Ernie finally grabbed my attention, laughing and telling me to hand the cigarette to Marichal, " . . . before he goes and kicks something. A madman waits for nothing."

On the first day of my life away from El Paso, I saw my first strawberry field. A field of wild berries, most of which were not straw. Make-believe fresas. I stood there, in the Tucson desert, reminded of the tree I had moved for my grandmother. Abuelita Kika had insisted that transplanting trees in the El Paso desert was necessary for our survival. Cousins Leticia and Fernandino had been snapped away from us too soon after the death of my oldest cousin, Gloria, the angel. Once, I overheard abuelita tell a comadre that one of the big agonies of my young cousin's death was that it happened on the day of her first period.

A brick building with a tall chimney startled me. It stood against the edge of my horizon as I inhaled the smoke of my strawberry dream. A door opened and a thousand miles of smoke poured onto the flat, brown, sunny landscape reminding me of the Plaza theater during a Saturday matinee. I always loved to leave the noon grip of a West Tejas sun and enter an igloo air-conditioned theater with a sky full of stars on the ceiling. In the early years of cinema, I had a joyful and constant career of attending matinees.

The baseball player with no name walked past us as we shared the mota. He grunted something about hopheads being worthless and spoke to God in four languages before he disappeared into the dust. Louis walked up to us carrying a jug of clear, white liquid. Half of it had already been drained into him, but he shared the rest with us. Ernie smiled and whistled to Jesus. "This stuff is hotter than my last woman." Jesús Alou swallowed his share and continued to stand in the batter's box. Juan said that drinking it made him want to throw his best stuff at the Dodgers. When I took a drink, I felt the desert sand scrape my throat. I coughed and choked, and my heroes howled. Ernie's eyes were gentle. He said I'd get used to it quicker than I could know.

I left El Paso, carrying a small suitcase filled with two pairs of pants, four shirts, a bunch of unmatched socks, and an extra pair of shoes. I was able to squeeze in an extra pair of shorts and one huge wool sweater. The last stuff packed was a writing pad, four pens, and six pencils. The ball players watched me write and a silence enveloped us. I wanted to write a letter home. Their laughter still rides on my shoulders. I stopped scribbling and we headed toward the main gathering of travellers. A campfire had been started and had become a magnet. I heard new noises and began falling into a foreign world. A world more bizarre and musical than any circus or band of gypsies that had ever passed through my West Tejas. A crowd of men were walking into the Sonoran desert. Men with no spare change in their pockets. Each knew when to leave and each knew when to speak and each knew they had given up on nothing. Patience was their pay.

The player with no name sat against a Tucson lightless sky. He was not a member of the group, yet he remained within sight of everyone. Ernie said those kind of guys don't like to be noticed. He asked me where I came from. I was shocked to be asked something so personal because from the time I straggled into their boxcar as the train rattled past the smelter on the west side of El Paso until this moment, not one of these travellers had asked me a question. I had been offered cigarettes, directions, booze, mandates, timetables, dope, advice on love, more advice on losing love, and simple quick responses to living, such as, "just keep jumping on the next train outta town," but not one of them had asked me a personal question.

I told the great Ernie Banks that I come from the home of the Chicago Cubs Triple-A farm club, the El Paso Sun Kings. He asked whether I go to many games. "Man, I tell you, if it wasn't for my stupid friends who get caught sneaking in with me, I would be at every home game. My abuelita knows two concessionaires and when I go alone they let me walk in with them. Whenever I let a pal tag along, the vendors get anxious and swear that it is not good business for me to be spreading secrets. Then they walk faster and when the guard notices the distance between the adults and children, he asks for a pass or a ticket. The beer vendors are gone by then and me and my stupid buddy get thrown out of the park. So I miss out on a lot of games by trying to be nice to my buddies."

Jesús stepped out of the batter's box. He overheard the conversation. He swung at my first pitch. "Listen, just don't stop being nice to your compadres. It makes a difference in war and in peace."

"What do you mean?" My shock had aftershocks.

Louis and Jesús spoke at once and Jesus backed off, letting the great shortstop respond. "Hey kid, it matters if people are your friends. It don't matter who you play with if you're running a game. You can win a game with enemies on your team. But you can't win friends with enemies as your friends."

Ernie coughed, contending that Louis was trying to make sense, but so far nothing does. We all laughed together. The cool night brought chills. I reached into my small bag and grabbed my huge wool sweater. Lawyers and doctors and sons of bakers were adding branches from the desert to a transient fire. Those without warm clothes nudged ever closer to the heart of the heat.

A red cardinal informed me that it was time to sleep. The party of roadside men stampeded into the night and no one had acknowledged any kindness from the night before. I lay on the ground, hugging my large wool sweater. Ernie and Louis said they were going to ride a train back to Chicago. Jesús said he'd wait for the next pitch even if he has to wait forever. Juan raged that his destiny is L.A. and that he'll send for his family once he beats the Dodgers.

The next morning, Ernie was gone. Louis was still sleeping and Jesús pushed Juan's shoulder, telling him the train was leaving. I grabbed my bag, not knowing whether to continue on to California or turn around and go back home.

Trains moved in a thousand directions. My head was tired and my eyes were cut open by a large scorpion sunrise. I jumped into a railcar that quickly gained speed and felt like I was riding a rocket. A rocket taking a child back home.

The bodies are in the air. We are alone. At least I am not buried. If the plane falls into the ocean, that might be all right. I think my body still needs to get burned. I hear something in the cargo hold. An airman has walked into our area with a guitar. He tunes up for a long time. I cannot yet communicate with the other dead. I want to talk. I am talking, but there are no receivers for my new language. Nana Kika used to remind us about how my dad had declared that the language of the dead is not learned until the body is given its final resting place.

The airman sings amongst the war dead. He is polite. The guitar becomes another singer. We are offered a delicate entrance into this new place where we dead must go.

X

A
Visit
to
the
Hotel
Cortez

President Kennedy was coming to town and the city went berserk. The Hotel Cortez is quiet and proud. The President of the United States of America will be staying in their penthouse. I have been a part-time dishwasher in their kitchen for three months. Bruce Cortez, my little league buddy, got me the job. Brucie's jefe owns the joint and his dad wants him to learn things from the bottom up. So Bruce helped me start at the bottom, too. Because we are only eleven, we are paid daily in cash and instructed to get the hell out of the sinks whenever the bell captain howls, "Just drop your aprons and go out into the plaza. Go play for a while and when the coast is clear, I'll let you know."

Bruce was the best third baseman in the entire Little League. He had the fourth best batting average. With the President coming to town, we're told to take a small vacation. But we still get to hang out at the hotel while JFK is in town. We just didn't have to do anything.

The President's plane landed in the afternoon. Bruce and I timed it so that we would disappear from baseball practice early and get to Five Points just in time to sneak through the crowds and shake his hand in the limo. We were determined that our pictures would be in the papers. Two Little Leaguers shaking hands with Mr. Kennedy. Too bad his wife didn't come with him on this trip. They say she was saving her energy for Dallas.

"Bruce, let's go before Coach sees us." I took my last drink of water before our great escape.

"Buzzy, stop being so fucking nervous. Coach will notice all your wiggles. I think he is already on the look-out." Bruce acts like he is tightening his baseball mitt.

I am pissed off. "Are you chickening out?"

"No."

"Let's go."

"Go!"

I never ran faster. We heard the vague screams of Coach, but we never looked back. We stopped at the railroad tracks to catch our breath. Bruce looked at me and grinned. I smiled back. We were happy. We were five minutes away from Five Points. We decided to run. Good thing we ran because the presidential entourage was moving fast. When we got there, the motorcade had already stopped for pictures of Kennedy with some babies.

We were wearing our scroungy practice uniforms. The President of the United States shook my hand and asked me what position I play. I didn't know why I answered, "I play left field." Left field and pitcher are the only two positions I have never played. Bruce responded that he played third base and the President's voice sounded like a baseball announcer, "Maybe someday the Orioles will need you as a replacement." I guess Kennedy could tell I didn't know what position I played. And that was that. The motorcade took off down Montana Street.

The finest things a grand hotel has to offer are all presented to the President. He stayed only one night. He was in El Paso for the signing of the Chamizal Treaty. The Rio Bravo changed course and clipped off a small piece of old Mejico. She wanted her land returned. So, Kennedy gave it back. Bruce and I ran wildly through the hotel. Because I was with the owner's son, we weren't held back from anything. When we got to Kennedy's floor, we stood guard with the Secret Service. There were three of them. One at the elevator and two at each stairwell. They joked with us that we looked like young assassins and if we didn't get the hell out of their way they'd send us to Leavenworth.

"For what?" I asked.

The agent at the elevator threatened that they will send me away for not being a good hitter at the plate.

"How did you guys know that?" I feel trapped. Now they do know everything about me.

Bruce chimed in, "How do you guys know that? Buzzy ain't worth a shit on game days, but man, at practice he tears them apart."

The south stairway agent joined in. "Because we have been monitoring you, kid. What do they call you? Buzzy? Well, for one thing, you are too damn skinny to hit anything with any power."

The elevator agent ordered us to go stand next to the south stairway. The elevator opened and a doctor and three nurses walked off. They were led into the presidential suite. The hallway was hot with silence. Bruce and I did not move. I don't think we breathed. A few minutes ago, the agents were clowns. Now, they were machines. Suddenly, even their skin changed. Earlier, their pores sweated in the heat. Now they looked like the soldier of fortune guys in Ricky Roy's girlie magazine pictures. These were tough guys.

I knew that Mando from La Bowie High and Jorge from Cathedral High could grow up to be like these agents. They had the same way about them. Mando once said he wanted to be a cop but then, in the next breath, he said that was too low of a dream. He wanted to go bigger. Jorge was the same kind of tough but he was short. Mando said the Feds would never take him, just the way the majors would never take him as a pitcher, because he was too small. "The scouts don't like chaparrito pitchers. They want them to at least look huge. Size intimidates. Plus, we are Mejicano bred. And that leaves us out of everything except washing dishes." Mando then slapped Jorge with a wet towel and they started chasing each other around the kitchen.

Mando's uncle, the chef, screamed at both of them to stop the shit. They both went back to the dishwasher. Bruce and I stood there, talking about what we have just seen. I asked Bruce a question, "Did you see three nurses walk in?"

Bruce gestured like he was smoking a pipe and

thinking hard thoughts. "Yes. Yes, sir, I did see three maids, I mean, three nurses and one doctor walk into the room of the President of the United States of America."

"How many walked out?"

"Two nurses and one doctor."

Jorge and Mando were wild with envy. Jorge was short but he was very loud. "What the shit! Are you guys halando our huevos? Don't be yanking us by the balls. Is this for real?"

"Sure." Bruce was the patron's son and they believed him.

Mando's uncle again yelled at all of us to cut the shit. "Brucie, cabroncito, you and your sissy compadre can just get the hell out of this kitchen. Stop fucking around or I'll tell your jefe. So just get out and let those guys do their work."

I got mad at the chef. "Why you calling me a sissy?"

"How many hits did you get last night against Odessa?"

"Nobody got a hit against them. They no-hit us."

"Yeah, but you still looked the worst. At least the other guys got some fouls balls. If you don't start hitting something, you're going to be lavando trastos, washing these same dishes for the rest of your life. And I will be watching over you on each plate. Not even your Nana Kika will be able to save you. How would you like that? Huh."

Bruce and I went outside into the plaza. We felt

like big shots because there was an enormous crowd lined on every street leading to el Hotel Cortez. San Jacinto Park (alligator park to us) was mobbed. There was no room for any new bodies. Bruce and I wore security passes around our necks. But, before we walked outside into the crowd, a ground floor agent advised us to stick our security passes into our shorts. "Keep them hidden. And stay invisible once you are outside."

No one noticed two Little Leaguers in the crowd of dreamers. The crowd wanted to sing to the President. Maybe give him a smile. Maybe share a dream. Maybe help him. It was a massive assembly of border town humanity.

"Brucie, look at that one, those are huge. Man she looks good." I stared at a woman who was probably thirty years old. She had enormous breasts and was blessed with legs that could walk across Texas.

"Buzzy, she's too old. She would probably eat your dick and keep it."

"Yeah, I'll let her."

"You probably don't have enough dick to keep her happy."

"Want to bet?"

Bruce spotted two girls our age and motioned for me to move quickly. One was dark-haired with short curls and bangs. The other one was blonde. She had breasts the size of the thirty year old. Her eyes were a new blue and she was exactly my height. Brucie started talking with the dark-haired girl and I began to stutter with my first ever conversation con una hueda. A blonde first girl and me.

Her name was Danni and she went to school at Loretto Academy. I told her that everybody called me Buzzy. "Danni, you mean you are in high school already?"

"No. Loretto goes from kindergarten through senior year. I will be in sixth grade next year. What about you?"

"I don't know. My uncle tells me that I should just give up on school now and go straight to college. But, yeah, I'll be in sixth, too. I have lived in this town forever and I was sure that Loretto was just a high school."

"Well, you're wrong." She smiled with a grin that said she knows how to be in many places at one time. Her eyes turned into opium. I was getting addicted to her.

Her friend, Yvette, was from Canada. She only spoke French and some Spanish. Danni spoke French, Spanish, some German, and of course, English. Danni was a military brat. Her dad had been stationed all over the world. Yvette was just visiting for a few weeks. They were trying to get a glimpse of the President. Bruce and I were afraid to let them know how important we were. After two glances at one another, we didn't miss a thing.

Bruce spoke to Yvette en español, stating proudly that his dad owns the joint where el presidente is staying. She laughed at him and mentioned that about an hour earlier, two soldiers had told them that they were here on special guard duty for their commander-in-chief. She said that they promised to sneak them in to see the prez. "So why should we believe you guys¿"

"Really, my jefito owns the joint. You guys want to come in with us. Buzzy, show them your badge."

"No. Man, it's in my shorts. Show them yours. I ain't taking it out here." The girls both laughed and said that we were even funnier than the soldiers.

Bruce pleaded with them to wait for us while he and I walked downstairs into the men's bathroom so that we could take those passes out of our chones. They laughed and ordered us not to be too long because then they would know we were doing something dirty in there. We got downstairs and the bathroom was empty. Bruce had to take a leak anyway.

"Buzzy, how much hair you got¿"

"I don't know. A little."

"You got any¿"

"Yeah."

"Let's see." Bruce turned around and I saw his penis. But I couldn't see if he had any hair.

"Let's see yours. I bet you don't have any."

Bruce unbuttoned his blue jeans and lowered his shorts. He didn't have that much hair, but he had more than I did and his penis was hard. I showed him mine. My hair was very fine and just starting to grow in. My penis was soft. He grabbed it and I watched it get hard. "Let's see whose is bigger when they get hard."

I grabbed his dick and we both tried to get ours bigger than the other. Then we put them next to each other. It looked like a draw. When we heard someone coming down the stairs, we quickly buttoned up.

The girls were talking to some big high school football players. We stood around and waited a while. Then, we got too impatient and started to walk away. Danni yelled for us not to leave. "Hey, I thought you guys were V.I.Ps. Aren't you going to take us inside?"

After almost jacking each other off, Bruce and I did manage to take the passes out of our shorts. I answered, "Yeah, we can get you in, but just you two."

The football players did not believe us, so they scowled at us. Bruce and I walked across the street back to the entrance of the Cortez and waited for the girls. They ran fast across the street and joined us. The guard signed them in as our guests, after he talked to Brucie's father on the phone. Mr. Cortez was in his finest hour. Granting wishes for those who have been denied. The guard commanded us to stay out of the way and said the big shot Mr. Cortez promised to kick the shit out of us if we got in any trouble.

We took the girls up to the Kennedy floor. The same guards were still on duty. The elevator one let us walk off the elevator and the two stairway guards started snickering at the girls. South Side said, "Watch out girls, because the little skinny one can't hit anything. And I'm not sure about the tall one. He looks like he could be weird."

North Side spoke his first words. "You young ladies look way too old for these little boys. You need to be looking for a real man."

Bruce shrieked, "You can go to jail if you try anything with these two. They are too damn young for any of you."

North Side mumbled a slow response. "You will never know how impossible it is to put us in jail. It would be easier to have us killed than to try and jail us."

Elevator gave North Side a look of contempt and then ordered him to shut the fuck up. North Side obeyed.

Yvette and Danni looked scared until South Side got decent with us. "What grade you girls in? Someday, if I have kids, I hope I have daughters that grow to be just as pretty as the two of you. Now, if I have boys, I sure hope they don't grow to be as ugly as these two. O. I would have to toss the poor things into a river or something. Hey, do you guys have any friends? And girls, how could you want to be seen with these two monsters?"

We laughed together and because the elevator guard was in charge, he promised us that he would ask the President for autographs for us. "But we must wait until after the nurse leaves. Do you guys have something he can write on?"

Danni said he could sign her bra. Yvette said he could sign her stockings. I said he could sign my shirt. And Bruce said he didn't need anybody's autograph.

Then he wished aloud that he had brought his mitt with him.

Danni walked over to North Side and started a conversation with him. It was hushed and I couldn't hear what they were saying. He wrote something on a card and gave it to her. They continued talking while Bruce, Yvette, and I traded jokes with Elevator and South Side. Elevator was as old as Mr. Cortez. He was divorced and had three children who lived with their mamma in Atlanta, Georgia. South Side was almost thirty. He had never been married. Too much travel. He said that he was only home about four or five days out of a month.

North Side looked like he was barely twenty-one. We didn't know because none of us, other than Danni, talked to him. They talked together for a long time. She laughed and he moved around her like a hungry bear who has found a river full of fish. Danni glittered in his shadow. They looked splendid. The river is green and fast. It is running with the waters from ancient glaciers. He finds the bend where the fish are pooling. He looks for her. He waits until she crosses his path. Large arms scatter the water. She was there. Her need was to become filled with his desire.

The nurse was leaving but she was no longer wearing her nurse uniform. What hair. Big, long, blonde and wavy in a strapless dress that looked like waxed paper wrapped around her. And what eyes. The precious eyes of a great one. She commanded more respect than the elevator agent. He obeyed her completely. She giggled at us. "Are you kids in line to see Mr. President? I just spoke with him and his back is hurting him very badly. You might not get to see him. But I hope you do."

The only operating elevator to the President's floor arrived and another agent escorted the nurse into it. She waved kisses to all of us and threw in a wish. "I hope he talks to you kids. He misses his own children very much. Bye. O, little girl with the blonde hair, you are gorgeous. Stay outta trouble, if you can."

Danni proudly rested her hand on North Side's arm. Elevator looked away from them and South Side talked with us as if he really liked kids. Once the door closed, the agent in charge suggested that it would be a good time for us to ask the President for autographs. He ordered us to knock on the door. Danni came running over. Leaving North Side with his mouth wide open. Four brats were knocking on the President's door. It felt like Halloween. That we would be greeted with treats.

Two giant agents answered the door. We expected the President. Both of them looked like the last time they smiled was at birth. Elevator gave them some secret kind of code, which must have meant we were all right. They allowed us to come in and sit down by the window. One guy looked like Sam the Sham of the Pharaohs. The other one looked and talked just like Wolfman Jack. We sat and listened. Wolfman grumbled, "Which one of you is the owner's kid?"

Bruce was silent for a long time before he answered. "Why do you want to know?"

"Because your old man said that I could lock you up if you and your pals get outta hand."

Bruce had grown tired of their stupid jokes. "You guys are so fulla shit. If I want to get outta hand in my place, I can. And so can my pals . . . in fact, if I want you guys to lick my shoes, you might have to because I got connections. And maybe one of you perverts will get assigned to dishwasher duty if you don't stop fucking with us . . ."

John F. Kennedy walked into the room. His Irish smile surrounded us. The smile that always connected him to us Mejicanos on the border. "How in the world did all you kids get into my room. I think I'm . . . I am going to have to trade all my Secret Service guys for Brinks agents or something. If they can't keep kids away from me, how can I ever feel safe." He gave us that smile that only the gods can give.

We were all standing at attention. Danni's blue eyes became an ocean. Yvette suddenly understood English. Bruce was rigid. I slouched with my grand question. "Mr. Kennedy, do you feel that the Rio Grande has the same significance to Mexicans as the Berlin Wall has to Germans?" I had practiced this question for a thousand days.

Kennedy placed his left arm on my right shoulder. "Son, the schools here are more advanced than I thought. Have you been studying European history already? What grade are you in? Ninth or tenth?"

"No sir. I am in sixth grade. I studied these things on my own."

"You are . . . I hope someday you become a politician. I like your style."

The President signed all kinds of things for us. My shirt. Brucie's. He even signed Danni's bra, but she had to take it off in the bathroom and bring it to him. Everybody laughed and laughed. Yvette spoke a few small pieces of French with him. Bruce talked to him about the stock market. Kennedy advised Bruce to respect his dad. "He runs a great hotel. Mr. Cortez is a fine Democrat. His employees are a sign of good ownership. They all have high praise for the way he runs his business. Pay attention to these things, son, they will be invaluable to you later on in life."

The president looked tired. He had smiled so much it almost became painful to look at him. We had acknowledged our president in our most studied and reverent way. The two bears walked us out of the suite. No other words were spoken inside that room. In the hallway, the shock kicked in. We all acted like car wreck victims. None of us talked. Elevator put us on the elevator. The only one to say, "See you later" was North Side. South Side and the old man both said, "Goodbye."

XI

The

Flight

Home

To: APO SF, CA
   Box 08444

August 30, 1968

My Dear Buzzy,
I miss you so much. We all need you right now. Did the
Red Cross get hold of you yet? Nana Kika died tonight
and I called them. I wanted to let you know right away
. . . Did they reach you? O, Buzzy, please come home.
Please. They said they might have some trouble reach-
ing you, but I know you get my letters, 'cause you have
answered all of them.xxxx

I didn't realize she was almost seventy-four. Did
you know that?

O, Buzzy, I miss you so much. Your Rosemary. Tu
Red. I laugh and laugh when I talk about you coming
home. I am going to play the piano (*like I know how to
play). I bet Nana Kika would just listen to me play because she was so patient with everybody.

love always. Red

To: APO SF, CA
    Box 08444

Sept 4, 1968

My dear lost Buzzy,
The woman at the Red Cross told us your unit is on an
"unreportable mission." She almost cried as she giggled,
"It is kinda like you don't exist."

    We so terribly wanted you here for Nana Kika's
funeral. Granny's magic was never the same after you
left . . . She kept trying to go back to the mercado, but
after you left, she couldn't walk without that stupid
cane. Well, one day I was talking with her while she
watched, no, no, actually, we were both watching una
de sus novelas. I can't remember which soap opera it
was right now. O, it doesn't matter. Anyway, she reminded me of the time you and Alfredo replanted a tree
for her in the backyard. She was so proud of you. She
said, "To this day, it is the only tree that keeps growing." With that funny look of surprise she gets when no
one else knows, she told me how Alfredo tried to dis-
courage her from moving it. He thought the tree was at
the point in its young life where it was too big to move.

    Remember Alfredo, our patron saint of the gar-
den? Nana told me all about him. Did you know that he
is already sixty-two years old? He still looks forty. I love
the way he looks—that dark, rough, desert skin of a
man wearing boots. That fine gift of his smile is always
there for me.

    Abuelita said it was the first time you ever wanted
to own anything. She said you insisted to Alfredo that

with your help, the tree could still be moved. So the entire rest of the day the two of you dug and dug and dug . . . first you had to dig out the tree. Then you had to dig a new hole for it . . . she said you were on a mission to get it all done that day . . . Nana Kika smiled that hilarious sonrisa of hers when she started to talk about how tired you looked that whole day. And Alfredo, with that miracle smile of his, moved along with you in everything you did, but faster because he was so used to moving through the daytime of a summer desert. Nana Kika said you were so used to moving through the nighttime of a winter snowfall . . . your having been born in Chicago must have caused this. She cried when we walked outside to sit under your old shade tree. You know, there's a bench and a pond underneath now. She looked up at the branches and cried, "Red, this is Buzzy's tree." All of us other kids our entire lives never knew that the most beautiful tree in Nana Kika's backyard, actually, I remember you called it the Southern Pacific's backyard, was there because of you. Your work gave a tree to all of us.

Buzzy, my sweet heart, please come home as soon as you can. Even though you were not here for the funeral, I will let you know what happened. I played the piano, of course. It made everyone cry. Then I asked Jimmy to sing "Amazing Grace." And when the piano playing was over, you would not believe what happened. I heard Nana Kika laughing and telling me that her patience with having to listen to me play the piano was over. Everybody always knew that Jimmy was joto. We all knew. But you were hard to figure out. I remember how I wished that you could be my girlfriend. And I always wished that I could find a man like you. Something about our border makes me want to keep crossing all frontiers. I felt your breath on my neck when Jimmy and I played the final music for Nana Kika. I saw Gloria standing next to Jimmy as he sang. I wanted to see you sitting next to me.

The services were held at Nuestro Señora de Guadelupe. I thought of all those times you and I took the bus with Nana Kika on Sundays when she decided to go to church . . . Nana Kika and you would get into these big discussions. The music stops playing and all I remember is me, you, and Nana Kika on a Sunday morning bus ride to that church. You would squeak at abuelita that this church was too damn far to go just to hear the servicio en español. You couldn't understand why St. Joseph's didn't have any services in our lengua. It was in our own backyard. It was surrounded by raza. What did you used to say . . . "Nana, with our country so full of indigenous and oppressed, why can't these Catholics make every church talk to us in our language?" . . . something like that. Remember how we all used to laugh at you when you would start philosophizing?

The priest was going to continue with the funeral program, but "my" uncle Martín and "your" cousin Ricky Roy walked up to la Señora Kika Soldano's casket. Each of them placed one hand on her box and the other on his heart and began to sing to her. Without music, it is called a cappella or something like that. The walls of the church have never held in what we saw.

Nobody knew that they were going to sing. Our hearts became tabernacles of grief as we listened to these hard men offer their soft voices to a woman whom they loved. As our abuelita from about a thousand lifetimes slept inside her box, two of her men poured her favorite song to everyone. "Cariño Verdad" from Los Churumbeles. Everyone has heard uncle sing a thousand million times, but I had never heard Ricky sing. It was the first time I ever saw them as beautiful. We sent Nana Kika away full of the love she gave us.

Buzzy, please come home. I want to be the one to take you to see her, O.K.¿ We all miss you. We all want our hero to come home, Buzzy. We are waiting for our misdirected angel to come back to us.

love, Red

Nana Kika was getting ready to visit la Señora Bustamante at the mercado. She fell just as she was about to open her bedroom door. She was almost seventy-four but I always felt like she was my age. Tío Martín was walking into the kitchen when he heard the kind of scream that means trouble. He ran to her room and she couldn't move. Uncle had to push the door against her body in order to get in. Her hip gave out for the last time. Many years earlier, before I had helped Alfredo replant Nana Kika's tree, I was the only one home the first time she fell. She broke her wrist and I carried her all the way to the hospital. Good thing it wasn't that far, because I sure got tired. The family always laughed about that story. They would recall skinny little me running three blocks to Southwestern General carrying wild, screaming abuelita. "I can walk. Let me walk. Buzzy, put me down."

And there is no moon left for you nana . . . recuerdo que mi lengua es de usted, recuerdo que me corazón es de usted, recuerdo que mi tristeza es de usted. I will never forget my language is yours, my heart is yours, my agony is yours, nana, and there is no moon left for you . . . in these hills that you never saw . . . recuerdo que mis ojos son de usted, recuerdo lágrimas, sonrisas, el sol jugando con Gloria. My eyes are yours. I remember to cry. I remember smiles, and the sun when it played with your tears as you promised me that I just had to ask God anytime I wanted to play with Gloria . . . there is no moon left for you nana.

The messenger is objective but I color him pale. I know what to look for. It is the notice of my abuelita's funeral. She was my mother for seven great and gentle years. She carried me with her from the day I turned six until I hopped on my first freight train from El Paso at the small age of thirteen. I am in a jungle, tightening the growl. The heat is different here. You sweat and sweat and stay wet. In El Paso, you sweat and get wet but you can dry off once you change your shirt. Nothing here can change the wetness. It is full of blood. Everywhere I look, en route to the villages, I see the lonely ghosts of these people's ancestors. Our unit prepares to move on and the message drops to the ground. Hundreds of blood-stained boots trample it into the earth.

XII

Poets

and

Listeners

Girls from the new side of town thought Chuey
Vargas was delirious. Chuey told white girls who asked
him his real name that he was "Jesús." They didn't
know that Chuey is a nickname for guys named Jesús.
He was a monster for his age. At fifteen, he grew a full
beard.

I first met Chuey at my cousin Sandra's quinceañera. It was Miss Baca's coming-of-age party. Everyone
seemed to be fifteen. I had not yet begun to shave and I
had never kissed a girl. Chuey was dressed in "borrowed" purple robes from the sacristy of the Iglesia San
Martín. His bearded brown face was punctuated with
dark green eyes handed down from a religious fugitive.
The first impression he had on many people was that he
could have been an escapee from a Federal prison. A
maximum one. His voice was purple. The first thing he
asked me was whether I thought Sandra could be saved.
I asked from what. He said from him.

Chuey, the mad prophet, wondered why I was the
only one who talked with him after he floated into the

celebration of Sandra's fifteenth birthday, yelling to the crowd that he could walk on water. My Uncle Nestor screamed at him. Sandra's younger sister, Pulgas, tried to bite him. We called her Pulgas because she acted like a flea. She never stopped trying to bite boys. Pulgas was twelve and already considered boys dogs.

Chuey's entrance left people stranded in mid-sentence. Silence, then loud confusion. I laughed and waited for the fury to die. Then I welcomed Chuey by handing him a stolen, paper-wrapped quart of Pearl beer. I had taken it earlier from the backyard where all the older neighborhood vatos and my uncles were singing and sipping and praying. Chuey, the Jesús from the south side of Zaragoza in the armpit of West Tejas, blessed me for my offering and thanked me publicly. Loud enough and mad enough for all in the house to hear, he declared that we should go outside and bless the old men in the backyard who were suffering for their sins. We glided outside.

Pito Echeverría, the west side's mortician, swallowed a drink of extra suave pulque and asked Chuey, "Vato, why you always fucking with that priest shit?" The men laughed a laughter sprayed with fear.

Chuey chugged another hit of la Perla into his Jesús throat and hit the hardened men with a soft response. "Because I love."

The silence was drunk.

Uncle Nestor walked into the silence and woke everyone by asking the young madman, "So, why'd your parents name you Jesús anyway? You're too loco to be anything other than un zero a la izquierda."

Young Jesús ignored Nestor and asked the crowd, "Any you guys ever hear of the poet, Pablo Neruda?"

As the group of small-town drunks shook their heads into the unknown, my Uncle Roman told me that if my dad were still around, he would know who this punk Chuey was talking about. Chuey tossed another one of his savior smiles at the negative nodding and pulled a small book from under his ecclesiastic robe. He began reciting, *"Cuerpo de mujer, blancas colinas, muslos blancos,"*

The men did not defend nor accept Chuey Vargas, but they did listen. Chuey decided to start over in English.

"Body of a woman, white hills, white thighs,"

No one made a sound as the gray eyes and the gray mood and the gray agony of the men surrendered to Don Pablo and his crazy disciple.

"But the hour of vengeance falls, and I love you," Chuey stopped to light a cigarette. The silent men waited.

"Body of my woman, I will persist in your grace.
My thirst, my boundless desire, my shifting road . . ."

Those hard men with bruised hands and swollen faces cried as the salt air from Neruda's poetry exploded in their lungs.

"Dark river-beds where the eternal thirst flows
and weariness follows, and the infinite ache."

Uncle Nestor re-sparkled the drunkenness with his

response. "Chuey is a great example of the infinite ache." Jesús/Chuey suggested that we not drink with the men because they would eventually get too mean. Some had already begun their cries about the horrors of their women. No. They had all begun to moan about the terror. The constant lament was opaque and brief. "She always wants something I don't have."

Uncle Nestor had too many quick answers. "You just give them what you got. If she don't like it, kick her ass out on the street. Then she can learn what it is to be white. Those gavachas just love pretending they can survive on the street. And all they want is dark cock and a green wallet."

Jesús interrupted. "Oye, Nestor, how do you know this?"

Then Nestor stumbled as he tried to punch Chuey. Too drunk to make contact, my bien borracho uncle fell against the rock fence. It cracked the skin on his scalp and suddenly the attention of the older men changed as they helped one of their wounded. Jesús stood there with his full beard and his crooked smile and his broken face and his fifteen-year-old soul, proclaiming "Nestor is not an idiot. He is just lost."

Chuey and I walked back inside the house to join the women and their young. Sandra smiled. Chuey and I were the only men in the house. We sat on the living room sofa, which was used only for special occasions. Weddings, funerals, and coming-out parties.

My Tía Yolanda and Uncle Nestor had three daughters: Irma "la Rubia," Sandra, and Pulgas. Three sisters from three different countries. Irma, at nineteen, was still the only natural blonde in our family. When we would tease her that she was from a wandering lechero, she would always answer. "No. Not the milkman. It was the priest." She was a soft and dark-eyed beauty with the funny colored hair. Our Blondie discovered early that her beauty could get her out of town. A film crew from the United States Information Agency was producing a local documentary on "Spanish" border towns. The producer promised a free ticket to freedom and she fell for him. Tía Yolanda declared that it was la Blondie's fault for getting in bed with a Federal agent. My aunt has always charged that the pain inflicted upon her by her eldest daughter was the most severe.

Blondie had no other name to us. But for the producer, she used her real name. "Irma" sounded funny when we heard that skinny tall gavacho with yellow teeth and a bald head call her by her real name. He looked to me like the pervert, Oscar, who owned the laundromat. Oscar was known for giving free loads of wash to any woman who was willing to watch him shake his thing in the bathroom. I remember watching him a few times. The legend of Oscar was that his thing was so tiny, he was embarrassed to put it inside a woman. But he liked sitting in a dark corner, shaking it and watching a woman touch herself. Eventually, the laundry went broke and Oscar decided to go to New Orleans on the Southern Pacific. But instead of boarding the train, he stepped in front of the lead engine as it approached the depot.

The Federal government film producer did not last long with our Blondie. She left the creep in Los Angeles after he introduced her to his third wife. Blondie was supposed to live with them in some weird mom and dad arrangement. Tía Yolanda was detailing the reason for Blondie's absence from Sandra's quinceañera when Blondie walked down the stairs and, without crying one single tear, sat next to Jesús, the young savior, Vargas. Chuey smiled and offered her a taste of la Perla. She swallowed loudly.

The summer before my second year of high school I changed my clothing style. I started wearing Tony Lama boots, Levis, and let my hair grow long. Wearing boots made me feel taller. And tough for the first time in my life. The hair down to the tops of my ears made me feel wild. On the first day of school I wore my shiny, burgundy-colored, ostrich leather boots, new, washed and shrunk, Levis, and my revolutionary hair. I was not allowed to enter the Jesuit-controlled building. My hair was "too long." I would not be allowed access to school until I went to a barbershop for a proper haircut. I walked away from the religion of my youth, never again to turn back in that direction.

The first two months of my second year of high school were spent following Jesús "Chuey" Vargas everywhere he went. On our first "school" day together, we stood on the middle of the Sante Fe bridge and "J.C." pointed toward the Franklin Mountains. Chuey and I had backtracked from his cousin's restaurant in Juarez.

Ciro's was our favorite place to eat whenever we crossed the border. Ciro never changed us. He told his crew to serve us anything we wanted. Jesús, in turn, helped his cousin learn more English words. We even got free beer because Ciro said Chuey was destined to become a great poet and teacher. He swore that someday Jesús, his primo a todo dar, would be a saint.

With our bellies full of Juarense food and Juarense beer we stood together under the bright sky. I felt contempt for El Paso. For the Tejas skyline. For the border guards that would not allow Juarez whores to cross arm in arm with me. I wanted to feel the same, but I did not understand the separation of skin by invisible lines protected with lethal weapons.

Jesús shouted at me, "Buzzy, look at those old rocky dirty mountains and then look to your right. Los gavachos have filled us with their right-handed history. When we look to the north, their homelands are always to the right. Right-handed history gave us anglo poets like T. S. Eliot who suffered to become something other than American. This vato Eliot was born in los Estados, but he spent his entire adult life trying to become an Englishman. His point of origin is not ours. He wrote all this shit and nobody knows what he is talking about, but the universities declare him a great poet."

I remembered having read the poem. "Chuey, the only fucking Jesuit at that school who was worth the sweat off my balls, Brother 'Honorary,' as we used to call him, made us read 'Wasteland.' Shit it took me a week to figure it out . . . but it made me feel so good inside about something that I didn't understand what that something was . . . so, does that make a poem good? What about Don Pablo? How did he react to this lost Americano, English poet?"

"Neruda could not stand for that. Don Pablo was more tuned in to Whitman and Walt's absolute love for humanity. T. S. was a liar. You're right though, his poem, "Wasteland" was great. After I read that, it was impossible for me to read anything else of his because I expected the same understanding. We never connected again." Chuey lit a joint.

"And some guy named Pound suffered because his philosophers led him back to the Nazis. Buzzy, we are not that way. Listen to Neruda. His heart lives in Chile. He will die in Chile not wanting to be anything other than a poet from the Americas. There are no schools in this town that teach us about Don Pablo."

I dropped out of high school when I was sixteen years old. And then every day seemed like a new summer. I did not return to Nana Kika's house. Granny had always said that all of her nietos were welcome in her house as long as they were going to school. "If you think you don't belong in school, then get a job and find out what it is really like to be out in the world on your own. And if you don't stay in school, mi'jo, that Army will take you and send you into war."

The sun was sartorial on the day I first went to work during a time when I should've been in school. My faded Levi's were stained with old paint. This old pair of pants and I had gone through a thousand-day nights. Yet, they still clothed me. The muggy room cradled us. I had moved into an unnamed colonia across from Sunland Park. To the south of us the border was now desert. The rio took a turn north toward New Mexico and from this dusty poor colonia it was very simple to get in and out of Juarez.

The roar of dust assaulted me and I breathed in a desert air coated with the eternal footstep cough of migrants. Freddie, the boy with no mother, saw me first and ran to warn the barrio that el borracho poeta has arisen. The truck that came to get me was loaded with bricks and a dented keg of beer. There was no ice and I asked what happened. Jesús (Chuey was attempting to abandon "Chuey" and go back to being Jesús) was driving, so he said, "Just get the fuck on and let's get the fuck going." I told him I was not jumping onto a truck full of bricks and warm beer with two idiots in the cab who don't know how to find ice for the beer. The laughter circled the desert rocks.

Jesús/Chuey had contracted us to work for his uncle as day laborers at construction sites. The old Chuey had also decided that he was no longer a poet. He had become a poetry teacher. He told me I had a talent and gave me some books on poor writers who had spent entire lifetimes trying to write, barely surviving poverty. But my life as a day laborer was brief.

Abuelita was right. I had dropped out of high school at the wrong time. The government had started a lottery for the draft and the first numbers picked came my way. I was not really eligible, because when I started first grade, Nana Kika had lied and said I was six when I was really only four. It was the fastest way for her to get me out of that home where some government agency had placed me. When the military called my number, I revealed that I was not eighteen yet. That my birthday was a lie. I explained I couldn't be eighteen because I had just left my sophomore year of high school. They said they would look into it. I called Nana Kika and she could not remember if there were ever any real papers on me. She said she would check it out. "Do not sign your name to anything right now. Don't accept anything they tell you. It will be a lie," she demanded. But I never listened.

Six months later I was spending my last day at Fort Bliss. I was at the designated turnout spot in McKelligan Canyon waiting to meet my connection. Instead, I met two women on the verge of a kiss which got me wild and high. I watched the two of them sitting in their car. I saw the driver's face. She was dark-haired. Beautiful from a distance. She moved like she was much older than her friend, a redhead. I stared into the soft desert air, impatiently watching them while they smiled at each other too much. I wanted to drown in the mystery of this mid-afternoon encounter while searching for some smooth "brown sugar." Mexican heroin is almost always brown and not very potent, but it gets the chivo done.

This was better than Scenic Drive, where all you can see is boys and girls kissing. Women embracing and touching each other between their legs is different. More powerful. Even after they spotted me watching them they didn't stop. They ignored me and I ignored the world around me. My only focus was on them. Only the three of us were there, sitting in our parked cars in a desolate canyon. I was convinced they would invite me to join them. But they didn't. When their desert fling was over, they drove away and glanced back at me with wide eyes and soft smiles. The car had California license plates. 444 is all I remember of the license number.

First Sergeant Ortiz called out two names. "Verbrosky." "Diss-a-shit." He was mean as ever and waved a signed requisition form in front of us. The form canceled the original request for thirteen more bodies to the Nam. Only eleven were needed. Sarge said it fast and hard. "This fuckin' gook war was not made for punks with colored toenails. You two have been omitted from the lucky list of those who get to go to the Nam!"

I wanted to hear the rejection again. Ortiz snickered that Verbrosky and I were now cousins. Overnight, the magic of rewritten requests had shifted a small numb numeral from 13 to 11 . . . Ortiz, my temporary god, said we were spared the trip to Viet Nam because the commander needed to choose the bones of white bodies for the end of the war. "Hell, all I did was close my eyes and point at two names on the list. The fuckin' war is ending. This kinda shit always happens. I been dropping guys names off the list alphabetically, but today I decided to change things around. You two little shits will remember my pretty fucking face as long as you fucking live. This shit gets me all excited. Saving the lives of little punks gives me a goddamn hard-on. You can give me a blow job now. I'm ready." Everyone, except Verbrosky and me, laughed. "Dismissed. Hey, don't worry, little sissies. I wouldn't let your ugly lips touch my dick."

Verbrosky and I stayed at Fort Bliss for seven days of Army limbo. We thought we would be sent to Germany. But counting bodies during wartime is a fickle game. Our new orders arrived on a Tuesday morning. Verbrosky was sent to Germany. After reading my new orders, I had left for the canyon in search of some brown chivo. I had been ordered into southeast Asia.

Inside this box, I am afraid those hauling me might not like sending bodies to be burned. Specific instructions on my next-of-kin paperwork detail that, should anything like this happen, my remains must be burned. A few of the many jokes on how to cook me bounce in and out. There is much to fear now. If they do not toss me into the oven, this memory will be stuck underground forever. I wanted to learn about Alaska. That estrella de oro in the north always pulled me. Golden star . . . no recollection that I have been there . . . except for a slight, insufficient suggestion twisting within. Did I meet a girl who once lived there? Nothing is certain.

The southeast Asian highlands rage with a crawling infection of gloom . . . A dark red nightmare. A junkie jungle exposing the litter of so many sleepless motions of growth. I want to hush the green silence of terror. A big rain drop slaps an erratic brilliance against a small colored dot. The heavy red crosses the green. O. O map my exploration . . . the last thing I see is a small colored dot and then a rain of brown and red across the green.

XIII

Travelling

with

a

Woman

Once the Army took me overseas, it was la Red who corresponded with me. Mostly, she could not bear the heartbreak of this sissy she loved being taken away from her. I answered Red's long letters with even longer ones. I sent her all my memories. And when I told her about my secret desires, she would write a story in response. I told her I didn't know the difference between porno and eroticism and that I was stupid with horniness. I wanted her to send me a smutty story with cunts and cocks and sloppy kisses and warm, wet bodies and the great smell of an orgasm.

Before the mercado got invaded by la Migra and FBI, I used to sneak into Red's room and slurp through her notebooks to where I found the beginning of another of her "silly little romantic novels." At first it was hard to read because her left-handed writing was so erratic. But after reading the first paragraph, it was impossible to stop reading. When I heard a door slam downstairs, I escaped by climbing out the window of la

Red's room. I walked quickly through the alley, trying to do something with my erection.

Cousin Red had written so much weird stuff and I was the only one in the family who admitted to having read any of it. I especially liked reading passages she was working on. She had recently been selling "novels" to a company that paid her in money orders. She never kept copies of the books around the house. Once she finished with a manuscript, it would get tossed in the garbage. She told Nana Kika that they were not worth saving because they were "silly romantic stories." They were written in English. Her pen name was "Lilly Crista." No one else knew this but me. It was another one of her rooftop revelations. The passages she left lying around the house were nothing like the ones she kept hidden. Around the house, Red would leave a lot of poetry and assorted beginnings of new stories. Hidden in her room were the real treasures.

Red was writing about a girl named Yolanda, and I told her that the story reminded me of the Yolanda who had kissed me before I got attacked by the Nazi mongrel. Red laughed and said, "I use anybody I can, Buzzy." Then she walked into her room and locked the door. She slipped some papers under her door so that I could read them.

I finished reading one of his stories about a woman wearing a pirate's eye patch and her sissy boyfriend and yelled at Red. "How come all your stories sound like I'm in them?"

Red responded by shoving another paper under her door. I picked it up and walked outside.

On the day the FBI invaded the mercado, everything inside came to a halt. Nana Kika was facing ten thousand soldiers. She looked grim. Her place was under siege. Maybe it was ten soldiers . . . it doesn't matter, they were all aiming large-caliber weapons at her. The first thing I did was kick one of the soldiers. He moved his elbow directly into my nose and left eye. I saw stars and a white light was wrapped around my whispers. I didn't hear Nana Kika's screams because I was listening to little birds who had voices of steel. Their sound was scratching my ears. The stars were moving in and away and my vision was blurred. I noticed that my hand was soaked with blood and that it was stuck to my left eye. I was afraid to let go because it felt like my eye would drop out of its socket if I stopped holding on to it. I heard la Red screaming. She had never screamed like that before. She kept telling the soldiers that they were all jotos. I heard a terrible noise. It sounded like a little girl's face falling on a concrete sidewalk. My good eye could see that la Red had just been shoved into the ground. A big anglo, breathing with rage, stood over her.

A week after the bust at Doña Kika's stall in the mercado, la Red and I boarded the Southern Pacific headed for Tucson. Nana Kika sent her to stay with our older cousin Socorro and I was her twelve-year-old protector. The rails were passing us fast and Red cried that she wanted to die. I begged her not to do it on the train because I was having too much fun on my first passenger train ride.

La Red, depending on which guy she was talking to, said she was somewhere between seventeen and twenty-six. Her hair was half carrot-red and half red-robin-red. Her face was gavacha pink and sprayed with fifty-two freckles. I know, because after the riot in the mercado, we both got out of the hospital together and she made me count them. I also know that she has 237 freckles on her breasts. That was fun. I lost count on her arms and legs and toes. She even had some on her butt. She didn't have any on her belly or around her pussy.

The day Nana Kika told me to go with Red on the train to Tucson, the brilliant girl la Red took me home in the middle of the day and took off all her clothes and told me to start counting freckles. She kept score until I got tired. She said that when she died, she was going to haunt that guy who got the raid started at the mercado. She was going to come back as a red-haired ghost spotted with the hundreds of freckles on her body.

The lounge car on the train was full, but when two marines noticed la Red walk in, they zoomed in to give up their seats. She whispered a fine "thank you" and we sat down. Suddenly, she was twenty-one and the marines were buying her drinks and buying me Cokes. One guy was from New York. He acted like that was important. The other one was nice. His hometown was

Green Bay, Wisconsin. I wanted to talk to him about the Packers. But he wanted to talk to Red. Both marines started talking at once and la Red just sat back, looking real relaxed, as if she had found some guys who would not get tired of counting her freckles.

The rails rolled by until my cousin got bored with me and told me to go back to my seat. I refused because abuelita ordered me not to separate from la Red. Then the marines turned on their "extra nice," offering me ice cream and candy. The one from New York even took out a dollar bill. I got so angry that I threatened to spill the story. "Do you guys want to really know why she is on this train?"

In unison, "Yeah, why kid?"

"Because she almost sent my grandmother to prison."

Red wiggled and smiled. "You guys, Buzzy has always been lleno de chistes. He just likes being a clown . . . Buzzy!"

The nice one was determined. "So kid, what did she do?"

Red would not let me answer. Her entire body transformed. From eyeballs full of flames, to fingernails embedded in my arm. Still, she was polite with the marines. "Thank you, guys, for the drinks. It really was very sweet of you to let us sit down. Maybe we'll see each other later. We have to go now."

In unison, "Are you sure? Can't the kid find his seat on his own?"

New York offered his condolences. "Hey kid, I hope you survive."

The nice one invited la Red back, "once things get settled."

The movement of the steel wheels on steel rails was smooth. The movement of la Red and I walking back to our seats was nice. "God, Buzzy, after all this time I thought I could trust you. How could you be so pendejo as to try to tell complete strangers what is going on in our familia?

"What do you mean?"

"Don't act so stupid. And listen, I wanted to get away from those guys anyway, and so did you. O.K.?"

"I know. Oye, Red, do you think Nana Kika will ever talk to you again?" I sat down in my seat.

Red started to answer, but she quickly threw a blanket over us, saying we should go to sleep. The rails turned into a lullaby as la Red put her arms around me and moved me to lay my head on her lap. She was wearing a short, dark-brown skirt. I rested my chin on her left thigh and she fondled my head around so I was facing the inside of her thighs. As she stared out the window, I stared into her skirt. The train whistled as it passed a small crossing in the night and la Red pushed my face closer into her center. I smelled the smell between her legs. The creation of desire. Slowly, she pushed my face against her V and rubbed her hands through my hair. She hummed a small song. Rails kept rolling. I stayed exactly where she had put me. She kept humming. La Red moved her legs farther apart and hummed me into her V. Her legs tightened. She sounded like she was trying to stop from screaming. I smelled her again. She was fresh and full of something I had never smelled before. I did not want this to end. The night rolled faster than I had ever known. Full of her gentle legs and her gentle brown skirt and her fingers in my hair.

In Tucson, Red demanded that I keep quiet about everything at the mercado. But I didn't have to. Cousin Socorro could hardly contain her disbelief when she picked us up. She was ecstatic. "So, crazy niña roja, what did you do to your pobre nana?

La Red was even more beautiful when she was embarrassed. "O, Sochita, nada más, but I will tell you it was not my fault."

Socorro, when she lived in El Paso, was known as the family newspaper. Anything that happened con la familia never got past her. She would find out everything there was to know about anybody. Now that she was in Tucson nothing had changed. She even knew about my involvement. "So, Red, y también you were using the Buzzy to do your dirty work? You were also using Buzzy? Wow, girl."

"Socorro, it's not the way you think. This guy I liked was using me and I didn't know it. Nana Kika hated the guy from the beginning and kept telling me not to do anything with him. She said que el era muy viejo para mi. He was from Chihuahua and a little bit older."

"How old?"

"Forty-one."

"Forty-one! Mi'ja, are you toda loca¿ How old did he think you were¿"

"Twenty-seven."

Big, brown, tiny Socorro, with tits the size of Tejas and legs the size of tall pines, and la Red, who was everything in perfect proportion, walked into the ladies bathroom together to continue their conversation.

I knew the girls would be in there long enough for me to take a small nap. I sat down on a bench and watched the people moving around as if they were walking into their own part of our tragedy.

"Buzzy, do me a favor, huh¿" La Red is holding a large box wrapped in old newspaper. I have just come back from an especially busy day of transporting supplies for Nana Kika's stall. Abuelita yells at Red that she can't send me too far because I will have to go back again to Don Martín's pretty soon. Red is the only girl Nana Kika allows to smoke. Red has a cigarette in one hand, the package in the other, and a promise from both. If I don't help her, she will strangle me. And besides, if I do this right I will earn some extra money. Fifty cents per delivery. Nana Kika pays fifty cents per day. But I'm not comparing, just thinking about how much money it is.

"O.K. But how far do I have to go¿ I have to be back pretty soon. Look how busy it is today."

"Listen. Go to Alfaro's pharmacy. On the side next to the pool hall, you will see a taxi. Number 4678. Can you remem-

ber that? Should I write it down? 4678." Red gets a marker and writes the number on an old rag. She throws it into the wagon along with the box. "When you see him, just give the box to the driver. That's all. Then come back."

The taxi driver in cab number 4678 looks like a girl but he is really a guy. 4678 takes the package and drives away. Red reveals to Nana Kika that she and the viejo have arranged to buy clothes for guys who want to dress like girls but are too embarrassed to shop on their own. She buys them everything on their lists and the viejo charges them double what they cost. They are willing to pay. Many of them are married, and still joto, but they hide it from their wives. Nana Kika tells la Red, "It is all right to pretend." And with one of her sneaky smiles, she says, "Not all of them are jotos." So Red better watch out because one of them will want her to help him dress up. La Señora Soldano, during various periods in her youth, studied with artists, theater people, writers, and gypsy magicians. She has never been afraid of illusion. "Reality is what scares us all, niños."

The girls exit their warroom with enough laughter to fill all of Tucson. Socorro, at thirty, has a college degree and worked at the University. She used to say the more she dressed up, the more those gavacho professors would chase her around. She would proclaim boldly that half of them were in love with her. Sochita never married. The longest time she ever spent with a boyfriend was three years. That was in college at the Texas Western. They graduated together and the gavacho left town with a million promises. He never even wrote her a letter. After that, we never met any of her boyfriends.

Cousin Socorro had a brand new car and lived in her own air-conditioned apartment. It had two bedrooms and a swimming pool. I walked inside and wished I could live there, too. But Nana Kika had her plan. La Red would be trained by our successful, college-educated cousin on how to make it in los Estados. Red said she never liked to read and she never liked to write and she never liked to study. We both knew this was a lie.

"This is not the remedy." Red was reading from a book of poems. I couldn't even understand the title. When she read poetry she always mumbled. "This fine concern invites all into madness . . ."

"Red, what the hell are you saying?" I woke up having to listen to her mumbling from a poetry book.

"Buzzy, child of no one, master of none, this is not the remedy." Red smiled and told me to go back to sleep.

Socorro walked in and laughed. Red was reading from a book a friend of hers had written. Sochie had three full boxes of his books. "You know, Red, you would have liked this guy. Pretty wild, but he was real smart in a way you don't find from those professors at school."

"So where is he?" La Red sounded destitute.

"I don't know. Rumor is that he went to either

Cuba or Bolivia. He disappeared about five months ago. The chota came to my house to ask if I knew where he was. Then after the local cops, the FBI came by and asked the same questions. They wanted to know if I was hiding anything of his. I told them that he had nothing. I don't even think he owned a watch. I told them all I had was three boxes of his books. About four hours later, los federales were back at my door with a search warrant. Esos pinches desgraciados tore my house apart. They looked through each box of his books and went through every page of each book. I know one of those gavacho queers took some of my things. Can you believe they went through all my things? Even my clothes. One guy wanted to know where I kept my dirty clothes. Cabrón! Anyway, I am missing one girdle, two bras, one I just bought the day before, and four panties. Can you believe those guys? The mean one kept asking about the title. 'Just what the hell does that mean? *This fine concern invites all into madness'."

"Sochie, did they come back again?"

"No. Once was enough for me. One of the law profs at the school heard what I had gone through and contacted the FBI in my behalf. He's one of the ones who wants me badly. He said he would represent me and promised to threaten them with a lawsuit. The only thing he said to forget about was my clothes. Whoever took them would never give them back."

La Red laughed and coughed and lit a cigarette.

"Do you think he would trade them for some bloody ones from your period?"

"Aye, Red, sometimes I think you are nastier than me. But you're still so young. Probably, huh?"

Sochita finally gave us the name of her poeta friend. Pablo something. She said he kept changing his last name. Part of him was gavacho, but most of him was Chicano. His dad's last name was something anglo and he started digging into his mother's territory for a new last name. Hers was Ruiz, but he didn't think it was poetic enough. He was trying variations on Neruda. Pablo Dura. Pablo Rude. Rude Pablo. Pablo Daneru. Pablo Aduren. She was not certain which name he took with him.

Red asked Socorro, "How good was he in bed?"

"I mean I never really did it with the guy. We would just go out together and drink beers and listen to crazy music and weird poets. He was great, but he never even made his moves on me. And then the first time I heard him read his poetry at one of those weird bars, I wanted to real bad. His words were beautiful and they made me feel so indecent. I just never knew when to make my movida. When I finally decided to make my movidas on him, he was very polite and agreed to get nasty, but he also told me that he would be leaving soon and probably wouldn't be coming back. So I chickened out. Now I wish I had done it. You would have liked him, Red."

"Yeah. At least he didn't fuck you over like that

viejo did to me. I wondered why the boxes were always so big for so little clothes. He would give me a list of different undies to buy. Always two or three nighties. Sometimes a skirt or a dress. But mostly panties and bras and stockings. I would give him the bags and then he would come back later with a wrapped box and instructions on who to give it to. It was always a cabby and one time Buzzy got lost for more than an hour and the veijo was all over me at Nana Kika's asking if I gave Digit the right instructions. What had happened was that Buzzy was standing a block away. Finally, he realized he was at the wrong street. The guy saw Digit running toward his corner in the rear-view mirror and made a fast turnaround. He grabbed the box from Buzzy and didn't say a word. But Buzzy got scared of the look in his eyes. This was the first cabby who didn't even try to look like a girl. He was fat with a greasy mustache and mean looking. If Buzzy had been one minute later, something bad could have happened to all of us. I never saw Buzzy so white."

"Red, I would have been whiter if I had known I was a drug smuggler. How much mota did I deliver anyway?"

"O. Shut up, Mr. little Digit."

Sochie joins in on the curiosity. "Yeah, Red, really, how much yerba buena did the Buzzy deliver? Boy, you guys were doing it for over a year . . . what, almost two years, no?"

Socorro and la Red left me alone on the sofa and

walked into the kitchen. I could hear them talking. It soothed me. They smoked cigarettes and drank coffee. I put my hands between my legs.

The next morning the phone rang. Nana Kika said I could stay over for two more trains, but that I must be back soon for baseball practice. This was the first time she had allowed me to play baseball during the summer. I told her that I could hop a freight that night. "No, Buzzy. You can wait. Little League practice doesn't start until next week."

Red stayed on the phone with abuelita for a long time and when she hung up, her crying got uncontrollable. "Buzzy, I am so sorry. Please understand me. I liked the attention that viejo gave me. He was always sweet with me when we were alone. Always. Buzzy, I am so sorry you got beat up by those soldiers because of me. At least Nana Kika didn't get hit. I got it pretty bad, too, but I guess I deserved it."

I embraced my most beautiful cousin and told her that no one deserved it. Then she cried even louder. Sochie came running into the room, demanding to know what had happened. Obviously, she didn't have all the details about how Red and I got beat up. The Feds eventually called an ambulance for us. When it came, I thought I was already dead and that I was just watching everybody for one last time. So did la Red.

"Goodbye, Buzzy. Tell Nana Kika that things will be all right now. Have fun with that baseball. O.K.? And thanks for taking care of me. When I go to Hollywood, will you come with me? Well, you have to, because

Nana Kika would never let me go without you." Red embraced me with all her fear and it felt like joy. She kept kissing me all around my head until the conductor laughed and said to either get on board or get loved to death. He grinned and stared at la Red.

And Your Eyes, Vague and Wonderful

you enter me

with fever

and high frail notes

of

desire.

the red

ribbon

from

a holiday

gift.

ominous

lights

form

a tunnel.

your

yes

penetrates

me.

we promise

to fly

like

angels

and

laugh hard.

a sad boy

trying

to be

worthy of

a warm girl.

mad and

noble.

—la Red

XIV

They

Came

Home

Before

I

Did

I never suffered as much in my entire life as I did during the two years I went to church regularly and tried to be one of God's children. The priests confused me. Three of the men in robes at our parish not only listened to your confession, but if you were a Little Leaguer, you also got privately blessed by them in their office. Because I played Little League baseball on a Catholic team, regular attendance at church was a must for starters. Attend church on Sundays or warm the bench on game days.

Johnny Renterría was a mediocre outfielder but he had an older sister who made me lose sight of fly balls when she was sitting in the stands. After Little League ended I did not see her again until a week after I had dropped out of high school. It was early in the morning and she knocked softly on my door. I opened the door into a darkness that held Elena's whisper. It was so harsh it sounded like the kiss of a priest. When you get a public kissing from a priest, it is always after he has made a lot of noise to announce it. He wants everyone to know his intentions are pure. So the racket usually has his bad breath mixed in with a speech about the beauty of God's children and the need to regain one's sense of eternal life in heaven by being kind to the children, especially the boys.

Elena's whisper carried the news that her brother Johnny was coming home dead. She touched my nose and I repeated what she had said. *Johnny Renterría is coming home dead.* A year and a half earlier, he had his birth certificate changed to make him look like he was old enough to enter the Marines. They made a medic out of a boy who was just one week over his sixteenth year. In those days, when this country was just learning about southeast Asia, Johnny was in the midst of its jungles tossing pieces of people into dark, thick bags.

Johnny was the first vato to teach me how to steal hubcaps. When I really got good at it, he was already over there. I would do my night work, thinking about how badly I wanted to let Johnny know that I was ultimately good at it. When he first showed me how to lift them and when I was the most afraid, Johnny whispered to me, "Just don't be too clumsy and too loud. You're supposed to be afraid. If you're not, then you'll get caught. Whisper through the fear that nothing can touch you. Whisper before stealing anything. Whisper to yourself that you will get away." I'm sure he was whispering to himself when the explosion in the Nam made his body look like a truck tire blowing up on the highway.

His mother would not allow an open casket because she had seen her oldest son's remains. His father broke wide open, screaming in the street. It was a scream that rang in my ears for a thousand hours. Finally, my abuelita took Mr. Renterría by the hand and walked him to the hospital. After that day, when I saw Don Pablo Renterría crumble into the arms of my grandmother as she guided him to a place she thought could fix him, I never again saw Elena, but in my mind I can still hear her whisper.

Manny Santiago reads the telegram to us. It states that his primo, Fernie Acosta, has been killed in action. We do a group sign of the cross. Then we make brave promises to get even. We decide to steal a keg from Acosta's warehouse, knowing Fernie will not be drinking with us at his coming-home party. The theft will be easy, because Manny is a delivery driver for his booze-man uncle, and he has keys to the warehouse. We walk inside the old freight-yard warehouse to find old man Acosta sitting there with the tapper ready. His crying sounds like a flooded river breaking a dam. He pours beer for everyone. "I'll pour the first one. After this, you guys are on your own. The first one is from Fernie." None of us talk for about the first hour, and then Turhan decides to thank the beer man, but Acosta tells him, "We all should be thanking Fernie."

Just before the sun rises, during the coldest part of the night, the bells of St. Andy's church rang. It is the choir song of sad angels leaping from destitution. Their angry notes fall into my drunk ears. In the desert of El Paso, these bells signal the return of another boy whose box will be covered with the flag. He will be given glory for his teen-aged death, for having fought jungle commies. It is early in the morning by the time we kill the keg. The big puzzle for us is old man Acosta. No one wanted to leave him. "We will stay borracho with you forever if you need us."

He ordered everyone home. "Hit the sack. A lot is going to happen in the next two days." On our way home, we stumbled through the cemetery where the veteranos were buried. No one remembered the first time he met Fernie, but each of us had a story of our last talk with him. The last time, in this time of grace, was all we had. My last time with Fernie was when we both went to Yolanda's house on Montana Street in Zaragoza. We had to take three damn buses to get there. The transfer at Plaza park took so long we had time to eat at Pinky's hot dog joint. I kept bugging Fernie, asking him why we had to go through all that shit when we could easily sneak into the Plaza theater and watch movies all day. But he insisted on saying goodbye to his Yoli and he didn't want to say it on the phone.

The bells stopped and I was full with the sickness of death. Abuelita heard me in the bathroom. My granny had always been a wise and soft wizard. She said, "More bad happens after the bad than before. And if you do not count your blessings during this nightmare, then your life could remain broken, wounded, and desolate." I did not answer. I heard, but did not hear her warning about Viet Nam.

Fernie came home dressed in colors, carried by

strong, sharp, colorful men. I could not speak about the ceremony because these things are private. Death is a very private thing. Especially for kids. The bad vibrated in my bones and I believed my abuelita was right.

Beto Garcia, my cousin Pulgas' fiancé was the first flag over the coffin. I still remembered the taste of her tears when I hugged her while she screamed. Then, Johnny Renterría. Then, Fernie. After that, they came back in rows and rows. So many that I lost count. Mando, my dad's best friend, and an old fucker who went back to their Guadalcanal days, came back just short of retirement as the casualty of a secret mission. Mando's nephew, whom we used to call, "Stoofo the scholar," was going to teach college. He came back the day after he got there. The young scholar's flag was bleeding during the ceremony. Flaco Leasure, my neighbor who said he was French, and the first vato to teach me how to kiss a girl, got it three hours before boarding the plane to come home.

Everywhere I turned, one of us was dying. Becoming a hero for my dead "compas" didn't take shape in the Nam. After my junkie, Crista days in Deutschland, I was returned to the Nam to finish my tour of duty. I was there exactly three weeks, three days, and three hours. Well, I made up the three hours. Ain't nothing that perfect in the army.

I will come home perfectly dressed in my dress greens. My medals for wartime heroics will shine like stars across a February winter in El Paso.

XV

Everywhere
I
Turned,
One
of
Us
Was
Dying

According to the United States government, I am supposed to be celebrating my eighteenth birthday today. The system had been lied to. But in El Paso, if you are Mejicano, they don't care about underage liars. They gobble us up like candy. My military career as a hero didn't take shape quite like I figured it would. If it hadn't been for Johnny Santiago's funeral, I don't think I would have gone. I allowed the U.S. Army to draft me knowing I was underage. Not that Johnny was the first. He was the one who finally tossed me off the bridge of despair. After his death I started to believe that I could go to war and return home as a war hero. Their families would welcome me back as a survivor. A survivor in a box.

XVI

Sky

Come

Get

Me

On my true sixteenth birthday, terror between my knees as I kissed Angie for the first time. Her boyfriend ran the druggiest gang in southwest Tejas. Not just mota, but real chivo. White China heroin. Belligerence runs through soft veins. Or, on discount, brown dirty baja, or brown sugar from Zacatecas. Chivo that would make you suck your dick. I wanted to suck Angie from her toes to her buttocks. She moved about like the movie queens move when their first film kiss is shown to an audience. She was more concerned with how it looked than how it felt. She was Red's best friend and scored some of his chivo for us. "Buzzy, if you do this shit, they can't take you in that army."

"Angie, who the hell said they were taking me? Are you doing this for Red? Did she tell you I'm going in?" I resisted her offer to get stabbed in my crotch vein. She called it that. It is the vein on the inside of the elbow. Angie hit it six times with her fingers.

"Stop. It's not working. Stop damnit. I want to go home."

"Buzzy, you are such a puke sissy. Listen. If those fuckers in the draft center see all these needles and marks all over you, they won't take you." Angie looked like she needed to sell something to someone. Otherwise she was going to lose her house, car, dry cleaning, status at restaurants, and her ability to protect the right from the wrong. Angie was worn out.

Sixteen months later I was in Germany with my army pal, Sammy. He was in a hurry and yelled for sugar. The water faucet was broken, so he cut the brown heroin with standing dish water. The sink was full of day-old stinks. He mixed the dirty water with the sugar, saying, "It will sweeten even the rats." This new stuff had an unknown potency. "If it works," he mumbled, "it will be cheap and sufficient bounty for the three of us."

Crista, his girlfriend and our steady connection, provided the crummy apartment. This was our postwar Germany. All of us in the 62d AD Hawk missile battalion had been shifted from the green steamy jungle surrounding Plieku to the cold snowy Nazi mountains surrounding a town called St. Wendal. Some of us were going back to the Nam but we did not accept that with each other. Sammy and I were in the first group of useless missile units to get evacuated from the Nam. Since the dollar bought almost four Deutsche marks, junk was cheap in this colorful world.

Crista had a soft voice and dark eyes. She had family from the Alsace and fucked for dope. Sammy told me of the many times they were going through a bad jones and she would go get stuff from Bargarder. Bargarder was the shit sergeant in charge of the NCO club. Sammy made so much money from selling dope to the troops, he bought a house for his mother in Brownsville, Tejas. He paid cash. But when Sammy stopped selling, he got pure into fixing. Sarge made sure of that. And Sammy always insisted that it was Bargarder who knew all the tricks. Sammy said that buying a house for cash was nothing compared to what the sergeant had done.

The stuff falling out of the tin foil was so brown it looked like dried blood on dirt. I watched Sammy fix. Crista was a sixteen-year-old junkie. She had been a junkie for three years and her favorite expression was that she would die young and high. I had seen her naked and it felt like a treasure. Sammy always said that if the dope got too strong, he could still get hard, but that he couldn't come quick and the women loved it. If they could get him up, he would go forever.

I peeped at Crista once when I wanted to score after coming down from the missile mountain. It had been three weeks. Sammy was on a temporary duty re-assignment. He was sent pushing to the south of Spain from Bargarder. I walked in and heard Bargarder telling Crista, "You look like everything beautiful I have ever seen." They were in bed in her room. It was the finest and goofiest room I had ever seen. The outside windows opened onto the main street, but there was no logical way to walk into her room from the inside of the house. The door to her room was a false window in the stairway. One had to know this. The deception was that good. In one of Crista's many panics for supply, she told me about it.

Crista's mother had abandoned house, children, dead father, memory, and love, and was living in Munchen with no desire to return. She left behind a daughter destined to frogs and foreplay for drugs. Crista said the false window was installed when her mother was a baby. She told Crista that not even the Gestapo could figure out where she hid and to make sure to stay guilt-free and quiet when the time came to hide.

Crista was doing Bargarder with her lips and he had his uniform on. Bargarder was the ugliest, stinkiest shithead with power I had ever known. I was too young to understand this beauty and beast shit. I stood still at her false window and watched him protrude into her face. He kept telling her how beautiful she was and to keep her fingers deep into him. As ugly as the fucker was, from behind, he had the nalgas of a woman. Curved and molded like the curves of a mother who has given birth to twins. She had her fingers sunk into his crack and I heard the explosion. His knees buckled and she smiled and wiped herself on his uniform. He stood with a limp cock over her face as she begged him to finger her so she could come. Ugly Bargarder stuck his tongue at her and told her he wanted to spank her with his belt. Crista asked him for some dope and he shot her up. Then he undid his belt and began to hurt her until she cried. She came with her knees shaking like a misfire and he walked out of the room laughing and commanding that she must obey him. "That is if you know what can be good for you, bitch."

The ugly finger fucker didn't know me. I walked out of the house before him. On the street, I watched him scratch his balls and give some dope to Crista's aunt. I heard him tell Crista's aunt that he was going to butt fuck young Crista next time she begged for dope. Her aunt said she would lick her for him so that he could slide in easily. His junk was heavy in her hand.

The rain felt like mud. The black German sky was spotted with the broken lights of dead stars. I walked fifteen kilometers back to base looking across their Nazi sky for my bearings home.

From:
APO NY, NY
     32d ADA 2/62nd D-Batt
     PFC Dsysia(Digit)

June 17, 1969?

Dear Red,

Hell, I even forgot how to spell my name and I no longer believe that we are really timing our lives by the number of the year. What goddamn year is it anyway? Feels like the dark ages to me. This old Nazi country is full of willing blondes and good dope. Don't know yet if I get to stay here and finish my duty or if I have to go back. Every fucking thing with this unit seems to happen overnight. Listen, over the past few months, I've had some tough dreams.

I haven't dreamed for a long time, but now that I am leaving Deutschland to return to the jungle, I want to know more about these dreams that I don't understand.

love,

Buzzy (Major Digit)

From: APO NY, NY
        32d ADA 2/62d Delta
        PFC Digit

Aug. 6, 196?

Dear Red,

This is the second letter but I am mailing them both at the same time. I am waiting for the fkn plane which will be another boring ride across the water . . . lots of hours and then I just touch back down in our country and go back to that sad, red, and green spotted country. My APO address will be the San Francisco one again, so write to me there.

When I get home, when I get home, we will sing songs of being gone, and when I get home we will dance. We will embrace the sun, in pink, small drops, into our red hearts, walking with the destiny of grace from a grandmother who left all of us a trail marked with the common goodness of a woman letting her children feed themselves upon her breast.

It is so hard writing to you because I have to keep trying to correct myself so that you get a letter without too many mistakes . . . but then with you that would be impossible . . . you know Red, it is very difficult to write to a writer because then all I worry about is if the grammar and shit is correct and how you will be disappointed with my poor writing skills . . . but at least I am getting the fucking story down on paper so that if something happens to me . . . Red, I keep having these memories and wondering if they are real. Do you know? My sisters are dressed up. I want to hold their hands and walk with them. They laugh because I am naked. Someone took me to their house. I'm alone with a man who looks like that viejo lover of yours who got us into all that trouble at the mercado, but it's my mother's lover. I hold his soft flesh on my rough fingers. I'm alone with him and he fingers my crotch. The girls laugh. My sisters are always laughing. I lifted him off of me when he was spent. My sisters shushed me to sleep so that I would not hurt. Lifting my shoulders and laughing at my long hair. Longer than theirs . . . I am dead so long from the day I walked away from nana and never said one word about her funeral, to anybody. Never left her either. She woke me up the first time I fell asleep in this southeastern Asian jungle. She helped me wipe off flesh from my uniform the first time I saw a land mine take away a buddy. She always kept something cooking on the kitchen stove, waiting for me to come through the door.

My mother letting me softly kiss her nipples, rubbing me to sleep . . . my mother touches me there in my most unknown center while telling my sisters that if I go with her I won't ever be happy. But maybe if we leave you with your grandmother . . . And I was weeping in the purple clothes of a widow . . . my mother tells me being widowed so young from your father . . . and I was weeping in the quilted night when I sinned with thousands of sinners, breaking our flesh against the stars.

Red you pull me from another memory but I am still remembering. Mail call Sarge announces your words on my letter to everyone in the unit. We are actually breathing salt ocean air for the first time in what seems like years. Those of us who still have all of our body parts attached act like it is the first day of grade school. Shy and excited. Memory ends.

Fear can so quickly turn to happiness. We respect happiness now, like it is the only thing worth moving another muscle for. Like it is the stop and end of our marching through green beautiful buzzing vegetation alongside hills and alongside mountains, and alongside villages. Everywhere villages with great-grandmothers speaking a tongue that was always theirs, and many times, lazy fingers dangling across the sky. Many times, as the others trembled and trampled across an ordinary village with no witness, with no one left alive to be healed by their ancestors. It or we or this or something that I will never see happen again is happening now. We trade agonies with small children wearing large caliber weapons. All the world includes me and all the world uses me, and all the world curves into my gentle moods when I knew I could be anything and when I knew I could fight for peace. But I could never fight. I would so much rather have kissed, held, wrapped around the sulky embrace of a welcoming smile, around the seductive shadow of my mother tossing her nightmares into the sky.

love,

Buzzy

XVII

Return
to
Sender

I can see Red. She is talking to Uncle Martín.

Uncle Martín, sitting inside his MG, tries to cheer her. "Maybe now we can have a party for Buzzy when he gets home. I just talked to that Red Cross woman and she said that the Army promised her that as soon as they found his unit, he would be sent home. Beside that, his time is up real soon, so they got to find him."

"Can I get a ride downtown?" La Red is watering my tree. She is wearing a short dark skirt and very light blouse.

"Mi'ja are you going to go like that?"

"Oye, tío, how come you only worry about my clothes when I'm outside?" She moves her hands across the front of her breasts and then sticks a finger into her mouth. She wants him to shut off the engine, call the bakery to say he will be late, and to take her downstairs like they used to before he started seeing his latest puta de Juarez. For Red, every Juarense was either a pig or a whore. Her vision toward her ancestors had been clouded by the white heat desire for her uncle. She did not want him to be a bachelor anymore. O. To be his bride. Especialmente, now that his mother had died. Red felt it was her duty to take care of him.

I was thirteen when Red and I celebrated a new year of hiding in the attic. We climbed up there at two o'clock in the morning and Red told me that she was sixteen and not a virgin when Uncle first took her. She said he always answered her questions with his erection plunging through thin white sheets. That bed and those see-through sheets seemed to first define his territory for her. She needed to touch him and so often after he had penetrated her he would so gently fall asleep inside of her. She had never known that sleep could be so kind. She said she wanted to be his baby, wanted to baby him, wanted to be his mother, wanted to be everything and every kind of a woman he would want. She said Uncle kissed her there and she suddenly knew that history was just starting and suddenly death would never be and suddenly the pushing of herself onto his big erection hurt it hurt Uncle but . . . even after he came we still kissed.

I see that Uncle Martín is impatient. "I have to take care of you, baby. If you walk around downtown looking like that, only God knows what will happen. When do you want to go back to work at the panadería? You know you can cashier whenever you want. Mi'ja, it might do you some good to do that again, and it could help take your mind off so many things that aren't going right right now." Tío Martín turns the engine off and jumps out of his tiny car.

Red wants him to pick her up and carry her downstairs, but he gets out of the car to see if there is room for him to start parking it under the tree. She gives up. "Well, if there is room enough for the Southern Pacific back here there is enough room for your tiny little carrito."

"Yeah, huh, the MG will fit okay underneath next to the pond. I can keep it in the shade when it gets too hot." He jumps back in and tells her he will wait for her to change clothes.

Red wants to cry but doesn't. "No, go on, I've changed my mind."

Tío Martín drives away and la Red begins to feel more uncomfortable than horny. She screams to herself. "He didn't even ask me why I wanted to go downtown. After all he did to me, he could at least care about what I am going to do." She goes back to her room to finish writing a letter to me. But I am dead.

The radio disturbed Red in the morning. She was yelling at me from her room. "Buzzy, if you loved me you wouldn't be playing that stupid Wolf Man radio so early in the morning." Red stopped yelling and asked me to go into her room. She was crying.

It was the November of my sophomore year at the Jesuit high school. I still worked my paper route and had just finished another warm and voyeuristic entry into Mrs. Triana'a bathroom. On this particular morning her hair needed combing for a long time. I stood outside helping her with each and every stroke. I helped her with her makeup. With her towel. With her nails. I massaged her feet while she sat on the toilet. I kissed her breasts. She pushed my head onto her lap and she let me feel the pulse in her thighs. Her soft flesh was softer than mine. Her lips were softer than mine. Her hair was softer than mine. The flesh between her legs was wet. Mine was hard. I left her combing her hair again.

I walked into Red's room and asked her, "Which boyfriend is making you cry now?" She laughed at me and ordered me to sit on the bed next to her. She was under the sheets wearing one of uncle Martin's white v-neck t-shirts. Her eyes were bright green from the tears and her hair was a strawberry red with the sun shaking loose the misery from her face. "Buzzy, go close the door and lock it. I want to talk with you about that viejo. That old guy that I've been seeing told me last night that he wants me to live with him."

I rushed back to the door and bolted it shut and told Red she didn't have to whisper because we were the only ones at home. Nana Kika had left early to visit with Don Martín and Uncle was not yet back from the weekend trip he took to Chihuahua. "Red, why do you even like that guy? Qué feo. He is ugly. Kinda like the viejo that always stays at Mrs. Triana's."

"Buzzy, you better stop peeking into her room. If that fucker catches you, you won't have any huevos left after he finishes with you. Besides, I thought I was the one you loved."

"Red, I love you in all the ways of love. What's it like?"

"Qué? What is what like? What are you talking about, Buzzy."

"What's it like to be with you?" I was sitting on the edge of the bed.

Her eyes said, "Move over here."

I moved closer and touched her face with my fingers. Newsprint was still on my fingertips and it smudged some on her freckles. She put both arms around my shoulders and pulled me into her mouth. We kissed. We did not stop. We stayed in our mouths for more than five minutes and breathing was shared between us, as the first small flowers of the morning sang to us.

When we stopped, Red told me to take off her shirt. I did. I had seen her breasts before but never like this. I put my newsprint stained fingers on her nipples. They grew taut and she pushed my face onto the center of her breasts and told me to lick either one. I started with the right one, went to the left, stayed on the left as she unbuttoned my levis and stuck her hand inside my pants searching to touch my pinga. I had never felt fingers so soft and so full of love ever touch me anywhere like she was touching me. And as soon as she touched me, it went soft. Disappeared. The excitement scared it away.

Red was not a puta from Zaragoza where you would get a rubber put on you by the "nurse" and then just run over to the bed with a dangling erection and stick it inside an old woman's twat and push and hump and listen to her tell you lies about how big you are and how good you are and to hurry up and why does it all take so long when guys have been drinking . . . "and listen, why don't you come by in the afternoon someday? Before you go drinking. Get your pussy first and fresh before all those other pendejos have filled my twat with their purchased love."

Red was the first real girl I touched and kissed this way. So I told her. I also told her that my pinga was conditioned to having a nurse check it for disease first. Red used one of her miracle laughs. It was a laughter she had borrowed from heaven. "O.K. Buzzy, stand up and pull your pants down and let me check that thing."

I was silent as I stood and dropped my levis to the ground. I stepped out of them and then Red noticed that I was wearing a pair of her old panties. "Red, I hope you don't mind but when you throw away your panties, I keep them. I love wearing you on me all the time."

Red shook her hair and flowers surrounded the room. "Don't worry, baby, I'll just give them to you from now on. Looks like we're both the same size. Come here, let me take them off you." I stood in front of the most beautiful girl in the world and she pressed her lips against her old discarded panties and made my small man become a giant again. She circled my erection with her mouth and the panties were crushing me with desire. She started to suck on my pinga through the panties and I started to explode. She stopped. "Buzzy, you're getting your panties all wet, take them off now."

We were both naked in her bed and kissing again and she tasted like the earth on the day it was born. Red directed my face between her thighs and told me to start licking her legs on her knees and then to lick behind her knees and then her legs behind her thighs and then on the front of her thighs, and then to lick between her thighs and to then reach deep between her thighs and to taste her wetness that was flowing out of her center and onto her thighs and I tasted the love that love was made with. She orgasmed with my mouth on her twat and she dripped into my mouth the cum from the old man. We were kissing when I first entered her and we were kissing when I finally got out, which was late in the afternoon. We made an imprint of this morning. We did it again three more times.

O. Green from forever. Snakebites and dancers with children in their arms. Green from forever. A Texas Sunday was invented for dancers whose frontier snakebites have receded. My daddy said that girls who waited for ships to come to port were the isolation that makes men dream. Girls. Think of it son. Fine girls in the Sunday afternoon waiting for a ship to dock. Not waiting for a priest to tell them that they have to keep from sinning. Not listening to anything. Men not listening to anything walking off their ship. Women, waiting for the first whistle. Waiting for the captain. A girl first listening to her lover undressing her. A soft cloud that fights with the sky. A rose in her early thorns. A velvet star. Cross my heart. Cross my country in your absolute desire. I returned from the war wanting all these things.